I thought our l[ives were safe.]
Perhaps they are.
I thought our lives were safe, but
I was wrong.

We came to the stone house in the woods beyond Mt. Baekdu after the Great War. My father fought in that war in ways that most people will never know.

Perhaps your father is like mine. Perhaps there are others like us in the world. Truly, I do not know.

I am Royameheir. My family have been Royameheirs from the beginning— at least 5,000 years. I do not know who you are or what you know. Perhaps it does not matter now.

The time is coming— Perhaps it is already upon us— when the secrets of life will be revealed to everyone.

I have been born into the cusp of this time, as have you. And so, you, whoever you are, if this writing has made its way into your hands, no doubt you too are being called and perhaps the time has come for you to know who you are and why you are here.

As for me, I am Grace Christianson, Royameheir.

# ROYAMEHEIRS*

*Roh-yum-errs

A pronunciation guide can be found at the back of the book

Copyright © 2015 by Melina L. Maloukis
All rights reserved. This book or any portion thereof
may not be reproduced or used in any manner whatsoever
without the express written permission of the publisher
except for the use of brief quotations in a book review.

Distributed by Amazon.com
Printed in the United States of America
First Printing, 2015
ISBN 9780996602808

# ROYAMEHEIRS

# Wind

By

M. Lee Maloukis

For all the Knights, wherever you are...
Especially Mason, whose whereabouts we always know.

Then a great and powerful wind
tore the mountains apart
and shattered the rocks before the LORD,
> but the LORD was not in the wind.

*1 Kings 19:11*

## Chapter 1

### The Meaning of the Wind

Sadness could never find a dwelling place in our home. Pain, yes, but sadness, never. For our hope is not in this world, though we care deeply for this world and all who live in it. A gravity came into our home that day – the day of the wind— that brought with it pain and with the pain— tears – tears that I and my parents wept, though we knew not from where they came nor why, only that something had changed the course of life. It was a malevolent wind that kept us up through the night, holding each other, and shivering, each of us being able to feel it, but having not the words for what it was. We simply looked into each other's eyes and felt it. A certain gravity was added to existence that day— the kind of gravity that only death can bring.

The day after the change in the wind, and in the midst of the gravity that lasted in this moment and continued on in our lives from that moment on, there came a knock upon our door. I remember the way the knock sounded— loud and strong with urgency. It was my first time to hear a knock such as this, though my parents had surely experienced it before. My mother was holding me at the time. She pulled me closer to her while she looked with a calm strength to my father and then at the door. My father stood up from his work, calmly brushed himself off, looked at us, telling us with his deep, brown eyes that everything would be okay, and then moved toward the door with a calm strength, knowing that whatever was beyond the door meant that everything would change.

Father looked through the round peephole he had carved into the door, as he always did, turned to my mother, showing her a relieved smile, and opened the door. On the other side was a sight that my heart recognized before my eyes could adjust to the hooded figure in the long, black cape. My father is a tall man, but Far Larkin, though only slightly taller than my father, always seemed somehow much taller. I heard myself let out a cry of laughter that matched the joy in my heart as Far Larkin stepped into the room and pushed the hood back from his head, revealing the dark black hair and twinkling green eyes that I could find in a roomful of saçèrdōtés.

Far Larkin was the saçèrdōté who, with the powers bestowed upon the saçerdōtum by L'Agneau, had baptized me into the life of the Royameheirs when I was just 8 days old, freeing my heart from the darkness that I was born into. Though my parents were Royameheirs, I was still subject to the darkness of this world when I was born into it, as all people are. I remember the seven days before my baptism and will never forget them. It was as though a veil was over my eyes. I could sense truth and the love of my parents, the knowledge of our people, but it was at this moment— the moment when Far Larkin, with his hands, poured the sacred water over my head, that I saw for the first time with the eyes of a Royameheir. The shadowed world was filled with color and love let out a joyful cry as it escaped my heart and went out into the world around me. All of creation rejoiced with me that day. My heart, upon seeing Far Larkin, always, and even to this day, leaps at the sight of him, remembering that moment of light, re-living it in his presence.

At this moment, as he stood in the doorway of the stone house beyond Mt. Baekdu, all was well with us, though the air was still pregnant with the gravity of the wind from the night before. He carried this gravity with him as he walked into our home. Something was different. The meaning of that wind was in his eyes. I could see it as he turned toward my unbridled laughter that was giggling out of my throat toward him. My arms reached for him, as they always did, and, as always, he bent his face down to mine, looked into my eyes, kissed my tiny hand and smiled as he said the words that would confuse me for some time, not being my name and not being a word I ever heard except from him, "My Reina," and then gave me the greeting of the Royame— he touched his forehead to mine. For a moment, as he did this, I could feel the power of the saçerdōtum in my heart and my mind and I always wished to remain there forever, but even as he stood up, the power of his presence remained with me.

"She's healthy," he said to my mother, his eyes smiling. Her blue eyes shone brightly at me, sharing the love that was between them— their love for me. He gently found my hand with his and held it. "What is it? Six months now?"

"Yes," my mother answered. "Six months."

"Has it been that long?" he asked, keeping his eyes fixed on mine, as though he wished to capture them in his mind. That was what I was doing, anyway... trying to capture every glint of light that played off of his smiling eyes. At this young age, I remember thinking, as babes do, that when he was gone, he was gone forever and it was the first loss I ever experienced. To see him return, my heart over-flowed with joy. All I could do was giggle and laugh at him.

"She is truly the most beautiful child, isn't she? She has your eyes, Gayle."

"Yes, they're staying blue," my mother answered.

"With your curly blonde hair, Steven."

"Thank the Lord that's all she got from me. Everything else is Gayle," my father laughed.

As my father approached my mother and I, Far turned and gave my father the Royame's greeting and then bent down to my mother to give her the same greeting. My hand went up to Far's face, surprising my hands with the soft, prickly presence of a new beard coming to the surface—a new experience for me. My father's blonde beard was always soft and inviting. They laughed as they saw my surprised reaction, breaking the gravity of the moment into peals of laughter.

Far Larkin unbuckled the breast of his cape and removed it, revealing the uniform of the saçerdōtum, the sight of which always brought me a feeling of safety and relief, no matter who wore it, but I was especially fond of seeing it on Far Larkin.  His black boots always shone like obsidian, which of course, caught my attention as a babe, but his black pants, no matter how far he had travelled, always wore a perfect crease down his legs.  His black shirt, like his pants, never wore a wrinkle or a stain.  The white sash that crossed his chest from his left shoulder to his right hip was also without stain and the patches that were worn on it, bearing in their various forms the signs of the Royame, which I would spend many hours of my life studying, were always well-attached; a stitch was never missing.  The buckle that attached his sash firmly to the side of his belt was always polished as well and would catch my attention for hours, watching the light bounce various ways off of the pierced heart surrounded by a royal crown, one of the symbols of the Royame.

    As the laughter ceased, Far Larkin's face again took on the weight of the information he carried with him.  He looked at my mother, searching her face for the meaning of its countenance, no doubt reminding himself of the strength that lay hidden beneath the exterior of her serene, sea blue eyes, then he looked at me and smiled, as he always did, twinkling the understand of our relationship between us, seeming to desire to stay there with me in my innocent wonder as he always did.  Then his eyes came to rest on my father, who was putting water on the stove for the coffee that Far Larkin always took upon arriving at our home.

My father took the cape from Far Larkin's arms and, with the reverence with which he always handled anything belonging to the saçerdōtum, gently hung it upon a peg protruding from the stone wall just to the left of the door. My father removed his work apron and hung it beside the cape, the sight of which always made me smile. Their work coverings hanging side by side, touching, always reminded me of the physical representation of the deep, underlying connection between my father and Far Larkin— one a worker in the Royame, one a saçèrdōté— a connection that had guarded the life of each in life, especially during the Great War, and would continue to do so here and in the world to come, no doubt.

No one wanted to break the silence. I remember vividly knowing this, knowing that they wanted to remain hidden inside this silence in a way and for a reason that they had never before wished to remain there in my short life. To this point, it had always been to prolong the unfathomable, undefinable moment, to not restrain the beauty of all that was, that would always remain unspoken, beyond words. But in this silence, it was something else... they didn't want to bring the meaning of the wind into being, wished to keep it at bay and sit in the peace that we all knew was possible for as long as we could; but it was there, we all knew. Whether we gave it its words or not, it was there. My mother nodded her head toward a chair, indicating a place for Far Larkin to sit. He sat, just as my father handed him his mug of coffee. He nodded a thank you to my father and situated himself in the chair, leaning back, resting his left ankle on his right knee as he often did, but then decided to place both feet firmly on the ground and lean forward, resting his elbows on his knees with his mug balanced between his two hands, looking deeply into the cup. His eyes remained firmly fixed on the coffee in his mug as he said finally, "Did you hear about what happened yesterday?"

My parents looked at each other, remembering every moment of the pain in the wind. We were living in the peace that follows tragedy, though we knew not for what we had wept. My mother closed her eyes and steeled her heart to receive the meaning behind our tears. My father looked at Far Larkin, showing him the strength behind his gentle countenance, which he could reveal through his eyes if need be.

Far Larkin looked deep into his mug again and said, "Ten thousand children were murdered last night in Maisondepahn."

I felt the convulsion of my mother's heart immediately, which seemed to take on a life of its own as the tears of last night found their meaning. Tears streamed from my father's eyes as well. The tears from Far Larkin's eyes, which found their way directly into mine, fell into his mug, no doubt creating ripples in the dark pool of coffee that, for the first time, would go cold in his hands. Saçèrdōtés rarely cry, and when they do, the earth can quake, literally. Rain started to fall on the window above our heads— great raindrops that beat against the glass individually, rapidly, one after the other. These came, in union with the streams that fell across Far Larkin's strong cheekbones and fell into his mug or spilled onto the floor, each raindrop splashing the semblance of Far's tears against our home, into the earth outside, into the trees.

My parents held each other. Their bodies convulsed, looked at me, took a breath, and went back into the pain together. This pattern repeated with the rhythm of the elements, seemingly. Then the wind came— a fierce, driving wind that beat itself against the door and the windows, trying to break through. It was another first wind for me— the wind of pain— of a saçèrdōté's emotion manifesting itself in the external world. I saw the look on my spiritual father's face as he seemed to try to control his emotion as much as he could, his coffee mug shaking in his hands as the tears streamed steadily into the hot liquid.

This was how I knew Far couldn't stop the tears... animals began to arrive at the windows, peering into our home to see what had happened.  They lived our life with us in the world beyond words that we lived together.  My mother's tears, upon seeing, in the window to the right of our door, the large, worried eyes of a deer she knew well, slowly came to a stop as she watched a squirrel appear on the branch of a tree and the masked eyes of a raccoon that peaked in through the bottom, right corner of the window.  They pressed their foreheads into the glass, seemingly wishing to reach us, to comfort us somehow.  Birds began to arrive and perch themselves in places where they could see into the light of our home.  My father, seeing my mother's attention fixed on the window, followed her gaze, and his tears, upon seeing the effect our sadness was having on creation and the elements, slowly stopped as well.

This is why I say that I know that Far Larkin's tears came from someplace beyond him.  Far loved creation very much and if he himself could have stopped the suffering of the world, he would have.  Though he saw the animals in the window, Far's tears increased, inviting the animals and the elements to take on this pain with him, to help him withstand it, so that the animals, who had by this time surrounded the house, began to cry with him and, as Far's body shook with sobs that came from deep within, the animals cried. The wind seemed to cry as well as it whipped around the house and through the trees of the Ukryty Forest that surrounded us, which began to shake, seemingly from their roots, rocking every way violently in the window above our stone house and around it. My tears, as I said, came with Far Larkin's. I felt his pain acutely in my heart and felt the tremors of his body go through my own. That was my connection to the one who gave birth to me spiritually. My mother felt my pain and pulled me close to her. I remember the pain in my heart. It was Far's pain. I will never forget it.

As Far Larkin's sobs seemed to be coming to an end and I felt my own heart returning somewhat to its normal rhythm, one last burst of pain must have ripped through his heart, for I felt it in my own— perhaps the remembrance of the cries of the mothers, which he told us later, could be heard for miles, even in the surrounding villages. The earth shook. A great cracking sound as of the strongest thunder was heard. It must have been heard for miles and just for a moment, everything in the house was lifted up with the ground beneath us and convulsed, as a final cry, beginning in Far Larkin's heart, ripped through the hearts and out of the throats of the animals. The trees beat their branches and their leaves against the stone of our house, the glass and wood of the windows, and into the ground; great drops of rain fell from the clouds, lightning crackled through the sky, illuminating the faces of the animals outside who, with eyes closed and mouths open, strained upward, pushing a sound through their throats that seemed to combine into a sound that would reach their maker's ears and then collided with one last peal of thunder that coincided with the last convulsion of the earth and the last sob of Far Larkin's body. Then all was silent.

## Chapter 2

### Into the Wind

As all around us became silent and the final tear fell from Far Larkin's eye to the ground, we all sat still in the meaning of the winds that had passed and the winds that were to come. Thoughts and prayers turned toward Maisondepahn, the little village to the west of our home, beyond Mt. Baekdu, where grace and truth had been born into the world. The little village, not much thought of before L'Agneau was born there, became the heart of the Royame and held a special significance for Royameheirs; therefore, it was always under attack by the powers of darkness. The

Royameheirs had fought to remain there, but the army of the Kiläl, the same army that swept through the town the evening before, had overtaken, by force, this sacred place. However, in the last two centuries, the Kiläl, mainly from the weakness inherent to their organization, had lost much of their power. By the Great War's end, Maisondepahn was almost entirely inhabited by Royameheirs. A renaissance, of sorts, had occurred there; hence the number of children killed in the massacre.

"Jonathan lives," Far Larkin said to my mother, knowing that this would be her first question. "Your sister and her husband took your nephew to your mother's home in Jordafsol three days ago for a visit."

The relief in my mother's eyes and her heart brought a small ray of light into the room. A tear of thanksgiving fell from the sea in her eye and melted, with the tears of mourning, into the damp, white veil that cascaded from the thin, silver circle that surrounded the crown of her head and washed down her hair and over her shoulders. The two sides of her veil always met beneath her chin and then fell like a waterfall, revealing the hidden mystery of her night-black hair and her graceful neck beneath its translucent, foamy folds. It was one of my favorite places to hide. To feel the moisture in her veil was unusual to me and I felt the coolness of it with my hands as I leaned my head back into it, sensing in myself the relief that was now in her heart.

Jonathan, my cousin, older than me by just a few months, was very dear to her. I had met him only once in our short lives on earth, but in that meeting, it seemed that I had always known him and loved him immediately. We shared one spirit and he was someone my mother loved dearly.

Inside this ray of light, my mother brought forth, gingerly, as though something in her swallowed the word as she spoke it, a name, hoping that this name could be added to the light that still remained on earth. "Justin," she whispered, the name of another cousin. Far Larkin looked into her eyes and, as sensitively as he could, shook his head no. Another name came forth, as she spoke another existence hopefully into Far Larkin's eyes, looking for the light and the hope on earth that we knew had been here only hours ago.

As I lay against her chest, I could feel with each name a pulse of life go forth from my mother's heart and into the world, healing it, somehow, no doubt. Each name became its own prayer. The three adults in the room eventually closed their eyes and said each name with reverence, offering them to the Father. My father held my mother as she said the names.  No tears came.  With each name, we entrusted them to eternity and prayed peace and acceptance upon the families of the children, knowing that in a suffering such as this, much meaning would be added to the world and inside this meaning, some life would spring forth.  Such sacred blood spilled on such hallowed ground must bring forth something of its own depth into the world, something as sacred and hallowed as that blood.

Added to the gravity of the moment was the fact that my mother and father had not seen, aside from my aunt and her family, their families in Maisondepahn in two years and would not be able to offer them the comfort of their physical presence at this time.  My mother and father had been shunned by most of those good people, though they loved them very much.  Such trials come in the life of the Royame and we suffer them as well as we can, but it is never easy where love and truth are concerned.  My father had led many men of the Royame into the Great War, but an evening came at a crucial moment in battle when my father left the war without telling anyone he was leaving.

Mezulari was a leader amongst the Melekorium, the messengers of the world to come.  Not often, but sometimes, if necessary, one of the Melekorium would visit this world.  Mezulari was a messenger well-known to my family. When he appeared, in the midst of the battle of Lys, resplendent with light, wearing long, silver hair and the silver-blue armor of light often seen in the pictures of the Melekorium, he asked my father to do something that my father would never do, except if asked by one of the Melekorium. Mezulari told my father to leave the battle.

In that moment, my father would recall later, he knew all that would happen. He knew that Mezulari asked him to endure something greater and more prolonged than physical death— the death of his reputation in the Royame; my father was a leader in the Royame and he would not be able to explain to anyone his sudden departure. Messages given to Royameheirs by the Melekorium are sacred and can only be revealed to few. But Mezulari was a messenger of L'Agneau, and so my father did what was asked. He was not ordered. In the Royame, no one can be made to do anything against their will. This is a sacred law amongst our people, but for my father, if one of the Melekorium asked him to do something, he took it to be an order and he left the battle. He told no one where he was going, as Mezulari had asked, and he took no provisions. He simply left.

He went to my mother, as Mezulari instructed him to do, and she told him to go back to the war. She did not understand how she could live an honorable life in the

Royame with a Royameheir, a leader at that, who had defected from the war.  She couldn't understand what he was doing there.  She was living, at the time, with her parents in Jordafsol.  The knock came at her window in the middle of the night, the story goes.

    She opened the window to find him there, hungry and tired from travel.  She gave him some fresh bread and wine to refresh his body, but then sent him away.  In sorrow, she remained with her parents, confused about what to do.  She loved him very much and they were meant to be married as soon as he returned from the war, but she could not marry a disgraced Royameheir who would not even ask forgiveness for what he had done and submit himself to the authority of the saçerdōtum.  He too was confused, for he had done just as Mezulari had instructed.

    Not being able to reconcile anything with my mother, he followed the next part of Mezulari's instruction, but without my mother.  He came to the place just beyond Mt. Baekdu, and in a clearing in the Ukryty Forest, he built the stone house from the Fontanna stone that he said lay there, seemingly waiting for him to arrive to build the house.  He lived in the Ukryty Forest off the land there and ate what was available to him.  He says that he never went hungry.  He built the house for him and my mother, though he received word only, through Far Larkin mostly, that when people realized that he was still alive, their hearts hardened immediately toward him, and this was the reality my mother lived with, bringing much sorrow to her heart, for she never forsook her love for my father, but it was impossible for her, at the time, to reconcile who he was with what he had done.

During the battle of Lys, the turning point of the Great War, many men in the Royame died, and the night that my father left, many of his friends were killed. To the wounds of my father's knowledge of this, when he received word of it, was added the fact that he could offer no solace to the families, as well as the knowledge, which became a great responsibility for him, that his own life was spared by L'Agneau, but the people he loved thought that he himself had spared his own life, heaping on himself, by obeying the request of Mezulari, the dishonor of the entire earthly Royame. However, no matter how difficult things were, he lived with peace in the Ukryty Forest beyond Mt. Baekdu and relied solely on the world to come for assistance, as well as a few faithful friends, but they were very few, and he relied on the word of L'Agneau, spoken to him by Mezulari, that my mother would be with him again one day.

Far Larkin was among the friends who helped my father while he lived alone in the Ukryty Forest. My father had offered his own life for Far Larkin's in the battle of Lys just before my father's departure, and so when the rumors began circulating about my Father, Far Larkin remained true to the knowledge of my father that was revealed to him through his sacrifice and knew that my father would never have left but for an honorable purpose, and certainly not to spare his own life.

Far Larkin recalled for whomever would listen, while my father was in exile, the story of the moment that he offered his life for Far Larkin's, as a way to help people remember my father's honor, which he had kept unblemished.  Gezur, King Maxamea's most powerful soldier, and leader in his army, had come from behind Far Larkin while he was administering the letzē rites to a Royameheir who was dying, to prepare his body and spirit for his arrival in the world to come. Just as he was applying the sacred oil to the soldier's hands, Gezur, completely covered in black Eiwengaarde armor, reached down from his black warhorse, Riðiðafhinuilla, equally armored, and with his large, armored hand, lifted Far Larkin onto his horse.

My father, seeing this, ran to the horse and commanded Gezur to release Far Larkin, though my father carried no weapon. When Far Larkin tells the story, he recalls the moment that he saw my father standing there, beneath the great horse.  He was relieved, he said, that someone had at least seen what had happened, but never dreamt that anyone, especially weaponless, would stand against Gezur.

He prepared himself to witness my father's death.  The next thing he knew, Far was standing next to my father and Gezur was lying on the ground beneath his horse.  My father had kicked the legs of Riðiðafhinuilla out from underneath him, taking advantage of the weight the armor added to the horse's body, and grabbed Far Larkin before Riðiðafhinuilla and Gezur hit the ground.  They both ran for cover together, having no further defense against Gezur, and watched from a distance as the soldier struggled beneath the weight of Riðiðafhinuilla's armor.  Eiwengaarde armor, penetrable only by specially crafted weapons, was very heavy and difficult to even cause the smallest dent in.  However, the weight of Riðiðafhinuilla's armor dented Gezur's armor to such an extent that he was unable to move.  Riðiðafhinuilla, having never fallen before in battle, was unable to get up.

Eventually, Kiläl soldiers came and retrieved them both, but with much difficulty, and their army retreated from the field for the day.  This was my father's last day on the battlefield. That night Mezulari would come to give him the news that he was to depart from the war.

That evening, while my father was trying to navigate his way home in the dark, the Kiläl army, in retribution for the defeat of Gezur, who was unable to fight without his armor, raided the Royameheir camp while they slept and slew many soldiers before retreating back into the night and preparing for the next day's battle.

For some time, the Royame believed that my father was killed in the raid, and gave him the honor due to a fallen soldier in the Royame. The Battle of Lys was won the next day by the Royameheirs. The Kiläl army lost its unity after the defeat of Gezur and began fighting amongst themselves, and the Royameheir soldiers lost in battle were honored; amongst them, my father. His death was greatly mourned. In the town of Maisondepahn, a tribute was paid to the fallen soldiers as well, and Royameheirs throughout the Royame descended on Maisondepahn to pay tribute to those who were lost in battle. My mother attended this service, knowing that my father was alive. However, she never revealed their meeting to anyone. She says that she mourned his death in a way unknown to all there, but she mourned him all the same.

My father, Stephen Christianson, remained hidden, unnoticed, in the Ukryty Forest for more than a year before a pilgrim named Gercek, of a tribe of Overlämnande, happened upon him. Gercek was a Demud Udi Aramad, a sand dweller, who lived in the Ketidaktahuan Desert; he was on his way to a shrine in Maisondepahn when, travelling through the Ukryty Forest, he found my father's stone home, which he had just finished building days before.

My father gave Gercek food and shelter for the night, and when the unknowing traveller found his way to the íljósi Inn in Maisondepahn, he described enthusiastically to the innkeeper, my uncle Samuel, the countenance of the man who had given him shelter for the evening. He said that he had never met a man so gentle and humble who possessed, in spite of his gentility, a strength that he had never encountered the likeness of in his life. He felt like he had always known this man and wondered if meeting him was not the reason for his pilgrimage. He was very excited about the encounter.

My uncle asked the pilgrim what the man looked like, sensing his brother's presence in the description, but not understanding how it could be. As he gave my uncle the description of his brother— very tall, more than 6 foot, with soft, curly blonde hair and a blonde beard, deep, almond brown eyes— my uncle says that the blood fell from his face and he began to lose his footing, for my father's family, along with everyone else, thought him dead.  My father had followed Mezulari's instructions without exception and my mother says that she sensed that it was not her place to reveal my father's secret to anyone, so she suffered the pain of those around her, including my grandmother, who thought that he was dead— in silence, a difficult trial for her.  When Samuel realized the person that Gercek described might be his brother, he asked the pilgrim to take him to my father.

In their meeting, a happy one for both, my father never explained, even to his brother, the full extent of the meeting with Muzalari on the battlefield. He only asked his brother, in front of a very confused Gercek, to trust that he had acted according to the honor that they both had practiced since their childhood and according to their father's teachings.  Samuel believed and trusted and helped my father secretly for some time.  My father asked Samuel and Gercek not to reveal his whereabouts to anyone, even their mother, and asked Samuel not to return if there was any chance that anyone would suspect where he was going.

However, my father would not be able to keep his secret for long.  When the stone house was built and was ready, Mezulari visited my mother in all his glory and told her to go to Samuel and tell him that she was ready to go to my father's house. She left her parents a note telling them that she had gone and to whom, but not where, and asked them to understand, trust, and not to worry. The excitement of being granted what she had awaited, to be with my father, was mingled with the bitterness of entering the divine shadow where my father was hidden, but she trusted in the powers of the Royame and its truths and was prepared to give up all she had in order to follow them. Knowing that my father was there in that divine shadow was all that she needed.

When my mother left Jordafsol, people knew that she had gone to my father. No other explanation was possible. Her parents never said anything, but people knew that she was not dead, and she was gone, so they put two and two together.

My father's reputation in the Royame was blacker than black when people found out that he was living, unharmed and alone, in the earthly Royame. But this was something the Royame in the world to come knew would happen, and even desired, for my father and my family, shunned by all men, were now protected— even from the good intentions of good people, which can often cause more harm than good, unfortunately.

The meeting of my father and mother at that time is the meeting that all humans wish for— to be assured of their faith in all things, to receive the happiness of life on this earth. My father received the reward of his patience, his faith, and his obedience, and my mother received the reward of being true to the love she felt in her heart for my father. Though he was disgraced, the love she felt for him never ceased, and she remained true to it until the eve of that happy meeting in the stone house. My uncle Samuel, at my father's request, bid Far Larkin to come to them, and he witnessed and led them into the sacramental bond of marriage that was bestowed upon my parents by L'Agneau and the Royame, bonding them for life, in this world and the world to come, as one complete being, a union indissolvable and sacred. I came into the world out of that love, that union, proof of that indissolubility, a physical sign of their spiritual union, a miracle of life.

Far Larkin, a witness to all of this truth of our lives, and our truest friend in it, as he sat across from my parents, his mug balanced between his two hands, his elbows still resting forward on his knees, tried to find the next words within himself. He knew our lives in the stone house better than anyone, that our life in the Ukryty Forest had been a safe haven for the mystical union that was the love that we shared. He had been invited into that love and shared in it in a profound way, and so he took the responsibility of his next words heavily upon himself as he said, "Stephen, you have to leave." He didn't look up from his mug as he said this, which may have indicated to my father that some conversation was possible. He looked into the mug, into the past, the present and the future, and he stated this as matter-of-factly as he would say, "The sun has set," which is what it seemed that he was saying.

My father, sitting with his arm around my mother and I, looked at Far Larkin, hoping, it seemed, to take the responsibility onto his shoulders where it belonged, and off of Far. He said serenely and gently, as was his way, "I know, Far. I am prepared. We knew this time would come. It is something of a relief that it is here. At least we know the day."

"The night," Far Larkin said, with the same self-assurance.

"Truly?" my father asked.

Far Larkin looked up from his mug now and met my father's eyes with the tenderness of a father and the compassion of a friend, and said, "Yes. I'm sorry. It's tonight.

You have to leave tonight. The Kiläl army has gone the opposite direction now, for today, but I do not know what they will do tomorrow. I do not know if King Maxamea will be satisfied with the blood of Maisondepahn. We simply do not know. There is speculation about the prophecy, as you know. You have to take Reina far from here, as far as you can safely go."

There was that word again, 'Reina'.

Everyone turned to me, as though they looked for some alternative solution in my eyes. Far Larkin seemed to search my face for an answer, perhaps another answer, for some time. My father and mother looked to me as well. Finding no other answer, they resigned themselves to the reality of the moment and the meaning that the wind had brought to us, and my father and Far Larkin stood up, offering each other the support that would be needed for the days and months to come, for we knew not when we would meet each other again or whether it would be here or in the world to come.

Mezulari had revealed this time to my father, as well as the place we were to travel to, in their meeting on the battlefield, so my father, trusting that all things revealed to him would come to pass, and being ready for them, had always stood ready for this moment, though he never knew when it would come. My mother was ready as well. She set me on a soft blanket on the floor and I watched as my father gathered provisions from the cabinets and carried them outside to the animals that were being made ready for the journey. My mother gathered things from our home as well, precious things especially that had been decided upon some time ago as the ones that would accompany us to our new home. My mother and father received the sacrament of healing from Far Larkin, to cleanse their souls for the journey ahead, and then Far Larkin celebrated the sacred sacrifice of the Missa, bringing the bread of the Presence into our home for the final time, and then consumed the bread of the Presence that always remained with us in our home, closing this chapter of our lives forever.

  Far Larkin held me close to his breast, as my father helped my mother mount Helmi, her beautiful, speckled grey stallion. My mother had traded her white veil for the black veil of the Bedouins, but her midnight blue sari, which she always wore, resembled a bedouin tōb closely enough that she needed not make any change to it. I remember thinking how beautiful she looked as she sat atop Heli, holding in her countenance and her demeanor all of the complex meaning of the wind— past, present, and future. A strength and a resolve were present in her that I had not yet experienced, yet she still remained the gentle flower that she would always be compared to.

My father mounted Kekuatansejati– Keki, as he was affectionately called— his black Arabian. Our mules, Kuat and Setia, were ready for travel. Far Larkin held me close to his heart. I reached up to pull his forehead down to mine, as the greeting of the Royame between us was always my favorite time with him, feeling the power and truth of the saçerdōtum in his spirit mingle with mine. A tear fell from his eye, which was a secret between us, but with this tear, came the sound of a lark and a gentle, cool breeze which brought to me a feeling of interior peace. This moment and these signs— the gentle breeze, the lark, and the peace that accompanied them were gifts to me that I would only come to know the value of later. I touched the patches on his sash for the last time as a babe and wondered at them, the symbols having had such a wonderful effect on my heart somehow, as he bent down and kissed my forehead one final time and spoke those mysterious words to me again, "My Reina."

He handed me up to my mother who had prepared a place for me close to her heart, hidden safely beneath her veil, and she placed me there with care. Far Larkin kissed my hand and my mother's hand one final time and bid farewell to my father, promising to look out for the stone house as he was able, and then our family, in the peace of the Royame, was ready to move forward, into the Ketidaktahuan Desert, which lay to the East of the Ukryty Forest, offering us the protection and isolation that the desert had always brought us to the East. Of course, there was Mt. Baekdu to the West, the Ocean of Perlindungan Tuhan to the South and nothing but forest to the North for miles. However, none of these could offer us protection against the mouths of men, who had already begun to speculate that we were the family that King Maxamea sought, and that I was the queen of the prophecy, whose progeny were meant to bring a long-sought period of peace to the earth.

Though Gercek and my uncle had kept the secret of our home well, the winds have a way of finding things and people had heard that we were here, though none sought us out. Most though, thankfully, still thought that we were not worth finding, and so left us alone. However, prophecies had been circulating for some time and those who could read them truly could find their way to our home, if they tried. We only hoped that those who could read them would have the integrity to leave us alone, and to this time, we had been safely secure, but how long that would last was always a constant thought for my family and Far Larkin.

A warm wind came, from we knew not where, surprising us, because it came from the mountainside, from the West, which never happened, and moved in the way we meant to travel, toward the desert.  We turned our backs to the wind and the horses seemed to wish to follow it, even before my parents were ready.  My mother turned her face in the direction of Far Larkin one last time, showing him the serenity of her sea-blue eyes in the reflection of the moon, which was full that night.  I moved her veil aside to find the countenance of my spiritual father once more, and remained there with him as long as I could.  My father raised his hand into the air, a gesture of peace and farewell to his great friend.  The semblance of his face, the last Far would see for some time, was an assurance of unity and truth in the Royame;  then he looked to the East, set his face firmly toward Misr, the place of refuge beyond the desert which had been foretold to him by Mezulari, and travelled forward... into the wind.

## Chapter 3

### WINDS OF CHANGE

The sorrow of leaving Hyamæa was present in my mother's countenance— not sadness, but sorrow. It mixed into the beatings of her heart, which I could always feel, being pressed against it, thankfully, for the whole of the journey. However, strength and a calm resolve mixed themselves into the sorrow, making me feel safe there. My father's horse, Kekuatansejati, always remained steadily paced in front of us. Keki's great, dark figure was a sign of stability and comfort in the darkness, amongst the other dark shadows. He seemed like a leader of the shadows, somehow, dispelling the fear that might be found in the other darknesses of the forest.

The animals who had been so close to us in our life at Hyamæa followed closely behind our horses, sometimes coming up beside my mother's horse, and pressing their foreheads against her leg. At times, she reached down to touch a nose or rested her hand on the back of her beloved deer for a ways. At times, if Skönhet, my mother's beloved deer, came close, I was able to stretch my fingers out and brush the tiny, white dots on her back, which I always found such delight in, especially in the dark, as they seemed to glow. Animals shuffled behind us— some, seemingly trying to respect our privacy, moved in and out of the trees surrounding our path.

My mother, once in a while, searched the sky for Pålitlig, the eagle who always kept close watch over my mother's life. Pålitlig appeared to my mother, she would recall for me often at bedtime, the same day that she met my father and perched himself in the tree closest to my mother, seemingly trying to hide himself most of the time. He would leave, but always she would see him at least twice a day, as he would find her in the morning and in the evening. Sometimes he would remain seated in the tree just outside her bedroom for hours; sometimes he would remain for a few moments and then be gone. When my father was gone to the war and then, during his time in the Ukryty Forest alone, Pålitlig was often with her, reminding her of him. My father saw him often too and was assured of my mother's health, he said, when he saw Pålitlig. When my mother's head turned upward and I could see the silhouette of her face reflected in the blue light of the full moon, glancing its light off of the the sea-blue in her eyes, mingling sky with ocean, I knew that it was Pålitlig that she searched the sky for.

  As I travelled through the forest in my mother's arms, I sensed the protection of the forest acutely. But protection, I have found in life, depends on obedience and careful listening, not a forest. As the horses carried us to the desert's edge, a small boat was arriving on the shore of the Ocean of Perlindungan, which had been the place where my father caught fish for us to eat. The men who arrived there wore the black coat of the Kiläl, though underneath they were dressed differently from each other. They saw immediately my father's fishing nets and the boat which took him out into the sea far enough to catch fish that could only be found in deeper waters. Mag, the one who carried no weapon, was probably the one who found the entrance to the trail that my father meticulously hid each time he entered the forest. Mag was the Kiläl who found such things as this, usually in the stars, but more often by means of the powers of darkness, which had led him to my father's fishing spot, no doubt.

It was not long before they reached Hyamæa, where they found Far Larkin casually reading a book of my father's in the kitchen. Péttur, dressed in an armor lighter than the Eiwengaarde armor used in battle, was still dressed, as the Kiläl always are, ready for conflict. His hand, covered in chained metal, rapped on the door of Hyamæa in a way, Far Larkin recalled later, that sent chills down his spine. He suspected it was a combination of the sound of metal on wood and the sudden understanding that the protection that Hyamæa had offered had been breached, as well as the fact that we were only an hour down the path and at least an hour away from the desert's edge.

Far calmly opened the door to the men, who fell under the protection offered to all men in the Royame, especially in the person of the saçèrdōté. He invited them in as he would any traveler on a journey and offered them a place to sit. Péttur, the soldier who travelled with Mag, looked to Mag for permission and Mag pointed to a place against the wall close to the door where he could stand. Far Larkin recalls that he felt sorry for Péttur, who seemed fatigued from their journey. He tried to offer water to him as well, which was also refused. However, Mag seated himself across from Far Larkin and received his hospitality with all the caution of a man who trusts no one and nothing but himself or those things he has control of.

"Would you like something warm to drink?" Far asked. "It's cold tonight."

"Whatever you have is fine," Mag replied.

Far felt uncomfortable serving Mag the coffee in front of Péttur, who stood against the wall, but followed the superior's orders, understanding and abiding authority, in all its forms. He had recognized Mag right away, but Mag would not know him from any other saçèrdōté, he thought. Péttur gently pulled back the corner of his coat, as he leaned himself against the wall, revealing his sword and the shiny, silver armor of his chain mail shirt underneath to Far Larkin. He tucked the corner of his coat behind him so that it would remain there throughout the visit and moved one ankle across the other, digging the silver tip of his Kiläl boot into the soft wood beneath his foot, so that the dagger on the back of the boot pointed up to the ceiling.

A situation of this sort is always difficult for a saçèrdōté or any true Royameheir, for they are sworn to tell the truth at all times and in all ways. But, as always, Far

Larkin depended upon the strength of the Royame, which he knew would protect him.

Far seated himself adjacent to Mag at the table, in the place where he was sitting just prior to Mag and Péttur's visit, but closed the book, which lay in front of him, and pushed it over to the side of the table. He sat, attentively, as always, to the man across from him, hoping that no judgment would betake him, as he recalled the bloody scene in Maisondepahn the evening before and could estimate with good reason that the man responsible for it was now sitting face to face with him— at the the table of the very family that he sought, but did not find.

"This is your home, saçèrdōté?" Mag asked nonchalantly, while trying to convey to Far the force and authority of the powers entrusted to him by the darkness. He sat the coffee Far had offered him on the table in front of him.

"It is," Far replied, having just had the home entrusted to him by my father. "You are a long way from home, are you not?"

"Why do you say that?" Mag asked, unwilling to offer any information.

"Oh, this place is a long way from anyone's home, really. Are you travelling?"

"Yes. We're travelling," Mag offered.

"Do you need a room for the night?" Far Larkin asked, hoping that Mag would be happy to be offered the relief for the night, but since Mag was travelling at night, he sensed that comfort was not what Mag sought. He was right.

"No thank you, saçèrdōté," Mag replied. "Which people do you serve, saçèrdōté? Isn't that what you do? You serve the people," he said, disdainfully.

"I serve people throughout the Royame," Far offered by way of an answer.

"Don't you have a church?" Mag asked.

"Not one particularly," Far answered. "Can I take your coat?"

"No," Mag replied.

"May I ask what brings you out this way?" Far asked.

"You may ask, but I may not tell you," Mag replied. "I am on official business. You understand that, don't you, saçèrdōté?"

"I do." Far replied, honestly.

"Do you know who I am?" Mag asked.

"I do," Far replied.

"Who am I?" Mag laughed underneath his breath, and looked up into Far's face, daring Far Larkin, with his black-brown eyes, to try to find the words that could define him, leaning his elbow forward on the table, and then sitting back in his chair, waiting for the reply.

"You are Mag, of King Maxamea's court," Far offered, making the most general reply that he could. He took a swig of his coffee.

"And?" Mag encouraged Far to continue.

"That is all that I can offer, having never met you personally until this moment," Far Larkin replied.

"Then what have you heard?" Mag asked, unsatisfied with Far's reply.

"I don't repeat gossip," Far replied. "It's a law of the saçerdōtum."

"The saçerdōtum," Mag sneered.

Far sat across from Mag, looking for the next move, thinking only that he would keep Mag here with him as long as possible, even if it cost him his life.

"Yes, the saçerdōtum. You seem to know a lot about it."

"Yes, I know the saçerdōtum. I know that you are weak."

"Yes, that is actually a defining characteristic of the saçerdōtum," Far smiled.

"You're proud of that, I see. And the laws you follow. They get you and your people killed mostly, don't they?"

"Sometimes they do," Far replied truthfully, without losing eye contact with Mag.

"Sometimes many are killed," Mag replied matter-of-factly, insinuating the massacre of the previous night with his words, inviting Far to the edge of forgiveness, inviting him to go past it into judgment and hatred.

"Yes, sometimes many are killed," Far replied, allowing the sensitivity in his voice, the weakness that he had been brought to over the last few days, to overtake the possibility of anger. He showed Mag, in strength, the sorrow in his eyes for the slaughter that had taken place, and dared him, in truth, to go any further with his questioning.

"You're not afraid of me, are you, saçèrdōté?" Mag asked. "You must not know who I am."

"Actually, I do know who you are, Mag, more so than even you know, I think." Far answered, hoping that some vestige of humanity's desire to know the truth still lurked somewhere within the heart of Mag, who was human after all.

Mag smiled and looked at Far Larkin, leaned forward toward him, and then leaned back. Péttur, sensing Mag's hostility, laid his hand on the golden hilt of his black saber, removed his toe blade from the wood of the floor, and stood up straight, waiting for Mag's indication that the saçèrdōté's time to die had come.  Far looked at Péttur with all of the care of a father whose son had turned against him in blindness.  There was something about Péttur that appealed to Far, though he couldn't quite say what it was.  There seemed a sense of questioning, an openness just under the surface that it seemed that he was pushing down in order to follow the life he had probably been born into.  It always exists, but sometimes it is visible in the eyes or some small thing in the manner, and when Far spotted it, his heart immediately called it to himself, in truth, and would die to turn that tiny spark of light into fire.  However, in Mag, Far had a difficult time finding it.

"Oh, you think you know me, saçèrdōté," Mag offered in the way of a challenge.

"I think so.  You are a man, the same as me, aren't you?" Far responded, sympathetically.

Mag was caught off-guard, just for a moment, at the thought that Far thought them to be cut somehow of the same cloth, and seemed, just for a moment, though no one but Far would be able to notice it, to find within himself the tiny spark of humanity that he had tried to extinguish, that he had told himself did not truly exist.  He looked away from

Far for a moment and into the cup of coffee, now cold, that sat in front of him, untouched. Did he see in the coffee that sat in front of him some sign of this humanity, and in its coldness, his rejection of it? Perhaps. For Mag was human, and Far Larkin knew it.

"I am not a man the same as you," Mag replied gruffly, trying to stare his truth into Far Larkin.

"We are brothers, Mag," Far Larkin heard himself saying, though was surprised himself to hear his voice saying the words.

"Even brothers hate each other, saçèrdōté, and if you knew me you would hate me, I promise you." Mag concluded, rising from the table.

As he stood and recomposed himself, Far noticed that Mag was a very handsome man when he was not hiding himself behind his hatred. His hair fell in long, polished, black curls to his shoulder and his skin was a deep olive color that he assumed women would find enchanting somehow, along with the sharp angles in his face that bespoke a certain strength. He wondered if he had ever been in love, since he knew women were attracted to tall, handsome men. He wondered what had happened to him. Then he pictured him as a Royameheir, as he was wont to do with anyone who had not yet come to understand the Royame. He thought he would make a powerful ally and sensed suddenly, perhaps because he seemed to have hit a nerve with him, that there may be some hope for Mag. But now was not the time. Though he had lost the stomach to look Far in the eye, Mag searched the room for Péttur, who could recall for him all of his power in the Kiläl through his subservience to him and his fear. He ordered Péttur out of the house and told him to ready their horses. Mag paused in the open doorway for a moment, noticing the eagle that had been following them perched on the branch of the tree close to the house.

"Don't eagles usually sleep at night?" Mag asked, eyeing Pålitlig suspiciously.

"Yes, usually," Far replied.

"Hmph," Mag responded. He turned to Far Larkin, sensing that the answer he sought was somehow very close by, but had been unattained. He began searching the perimeter with his eyes, relying on his human senses, since his ability to ascertain underlying realities seemed to be somewhat dampened in the saçèrdōté's presence.

"Where are your other animals?" Mag asked, finding a renewed strength to look Far Larkin in the eyes.

"I have no other animals but the mare you see in the stable," Far replied truthfully, as his heart began to beat sensibly in his chest, sensing the mystery of his friends' existence giving way very quickly to the evil of the present moment.

"There were other animals here," Mag replied, gaining strength, as he left Far's side, threw open the door, and made his way to the stables, inspecting the feed troughs and the buckets that still contained fresh feed and water.

He came back and stood squarely in front of Far, searching his eyes for the answers he was looking for.

"I should kill you," Mag spoke into Far Larkin's face.

Péttur returned from the stables, drawing his sword, and pointing the tip of the blade at Far's neck. "By the stables and the horse prints, I would say that they've been gone for about an hour," Péttur said, leaving his sword poised against the soft spot at the base of Far Larkin's neck.

"Why?" Far Larkin asked calmly.

"For obstructing the king's justice," Mag replied.

"Justice?" Far Larkin questioned him, never moving his eyes from Mag's. "Do you know what justice is, Mag?"

"It's what I say it is, saçèrdōté." Mag spat, grabbing Far's chin with his hand, squeezing it upward, trying to force him into at least physical agreement that his justice existed and Far was at the mercy of it, whether he believed in it or not.

"What do you want to do with him, sire?" Péttur asked, looking from Far Larkin to Mag, and back again.

Mag looked deep into Far's eyes, daring Far to invite his own death upon himself, but thought that Far might be more powerful dead than alive, since this was one of the tenants of his own belief.

"Leave him here," Mag said to Péttur, loosening his grip on Far's face.  He took Péttur's sword from his hand, poised it over Far Larkin's head as though ready to strike and said, "Break his legs," leaving Péttur to do the dirty work alone.  "Follow the trail when you are able.  Find me!" Mag shouted at Péttur, as he mounted Far's horse, Heiður, and then galloped down the trail of hoof prints, into the forest, his long black coat lifted up and trailing behind him in the wind of his speed.

Far Larkin and Péttur both watched, Péttur now feeling somewhat vulnerable without his sword, as Pålitlig swiftly mounted the air, flew past Mag, and lifted himself up into the currents of air, marking his eagle's heart for my mother, and soaring toward us as fast as his wings would carry him.

We were riding rather slowly down the path when Pålitlig came up from behind Heli and soared past my mother's right shoulder, and then my father's.  My father's horse stopped as he looked back to my mother, searching her face for an answer. We all stopped. I lifted my head up out of my mother's veil, sensing that something was happening. I laughed, as always, when I saw Pålitlig, pointed up in the sky, and smiled, trying to follow him as I often did when I had lain on my blanket on the ground in front of Hyamæa. Pålitlig would soar in the sky above my head for hours at times if I was outside, and would dance for me often until it was time for him to go home to the cave where he lived with his family. One of my favorite memories is of Pålitlig circling the air with his mate, grabbing her claws, and tumbling with her through the air, coming so close to me that I could feel the wind of their feathers brush past me, and then fly up into the air again.

    I watched as Pålitlig flew up into the air in front of my father, turned around, came from the back, behind Heli and my mother, and flew forward again, past my mother's shoulder. We felt the wind of Pålitlig's wings rushing past, as he flew forward to my father, and this time, went forward into the forest, seemingly getting lost in the foliage and the darkness ahead of us. He did this again. Each time, I giggled with laughter, happy to see Pålitlig so close, and so fast, feeling the rush of Pålitlig's wings against my skin, but my mother and father exchanged a look of knowing between themselves. My father never said anything. He got off of his horse, made sure that all of the items tied to the horses and Kuat and Setia were secured, he walked over to Heli and leaned his head into my mother's lap, as I found his blonde beard and felt the silkiness of his curls, smiled into his face, found a smile in his, and pulled his forehead toward mine, remaining there for a moment. My mother bent down to give him a kiss, and then he mounted his horse, and, as fast as we could, we followed Pålitlig into the forest, toward the desert wind.

## Chapter 4

## Desert Wind

We knew not what evil hunted us as we made our way to the edge of the desert, but we trusted in Pålitlig's warning and travelled as quickly as we were able. My father and mother knew that we travelled under the protection of the Royame and knew that the Melekorium would assist us in whatever way they were able; however, I could feel my mother's heartbeat increase with the speed of our horses. Setia and Kuat struggled to keep up with us, but they slowed us down immensely.

My father, sensing the present danger, stopped suddenly and dismounted Keki. He took a few precious things that the mules carried and placed them in his own saddlebags and the saddlebags of my mother's horse, Heli. He then took the rest of the things that we had placed on their backs and hid them in the nook of a tree, covered them well, and sent Kuat and Setia into the forest with the other animals who were keeping pace with us. My father came to give us another kiss, quickly, and then he mounted Keki again, as my mother and I bid farewell to our beloved mules, and then we flew.

I had never travelled so fast before. For me, it was exhilerating. I felt the rockiness of a fast trot ease itself into the glide of a gallop and it seemed that Heli was not even moving, yet we were travelling at great speed. Three deer and a lion kept pace with us so that it seemed that we were part of a mixed herd travelling through the mostly-unmarked trail of the forest that my father knew so well. At times, the trail widened so that Keki and Heli were side by side and I could see my father's midnight-blue coat flying beside us in the wind. At other times the trail narrowed so that we were all in a single line, with the lion, whom my mother had named Roi, at the back. I knew the wind well and had always wished to be inside it, but now it was as if we were truly inside the wind. Still, I know now, we could not have travelled as fast as Mag, who rode Far Larkin's midnight-black mare, Heiður, prized for her agility and speed, and her courage.

We travelled like that for some time, breaking twigs off the branches of trees that we passed as though they were icicles, feeling the heat of the deer who flanked us on either side at times, seeing my father's blonde hair like a bolt of lightning under the light of the full moon, which could be seen, it seemed, almost always. After some time, I noticed a change in the light. It became brighter. My mother's face was lit blue, and I could make out the details of my father's figure, which had mostly been shadow until this point. We were nearing the break in the forest, where it began to give way to open land, which led quickly into the desert. It was in the midst of this newfound light that we began to hear unfamiliar hoofbeats coming from behind us. I noticed them. They sounded like the hoofbeats of Keki and Heli, which were distinctly different from the hoofbeats of the deer and, especially Roi. I saw my mother's face as she looked back behind her, and then she rode up next to my father and motioned for him to look back.

Mag was closing in fast as he waved Péttur's sword around his head at something in the air. Pålitlig had been trying to knock him to the ground. However, a great, blue-black crow, certainly called out of the forest by Mag, was distracting Pålitlig from his target. The crow and Pålitlig, at times, flew into the space in front of us, as they locked claws and tumbled through the air, catching each other's feathers in their beaks, and then, having split apart just before hitting the ground, found their ways into the air again.

Pålitlig was always trying to navigate himself toward Mag, seemingly hoping to knock him from Heiður's back. However, Mag's crow was never far behind, and would intercept Pålitlig usually before he was able to make contact with Mag, though he did manage to wrap a wing around Mag's face a few times, causing Mag to yell in a way I had never heard a human yell before. This was my first introduction to hatred. It confused me, I remember— the violence. I didn't understand it at first; it was so different from what I was used to seeing from a human. I think it wasn't until much later that I actually realized that Mag was human. I thought that he was another type of animal – one who could ride a horse, though I had never seen an animal act that way either. I didn't really know what he was.

Suddenly, as though a curtain was pulled, we were out of the forest and driving forward, the five of us, on open, sandy, land that was speckled with little bushes here and there. We moved faster and faster toward the desert, but in the openess of the land, Mag was able to take advantage of his lightness, for he had no baby to take care of, and Heiður's speed to carry him. Three deer flanked us on either side and in the back, protectively, so that Mag was unable to get too close. Roi, unfortunately, had fallen behind all the horses, not being built for that kind of speed over such a long distance.

Mag brandished his iron at Trinidad, the deer who kept close to my mother's right side, so that once in a while she had to fall back just enough that Mag was able to come very close to Heli, but before he could reach her, Trinidad would run up between them, separating Mag from my mother. When Mag saw that he would be unable to reach my mother, he set his sights on my father and began to move forward toward him.

Perhaps it was with the aid of the Melekorium, because my mother says that she has never seen a lion move so fast and did not know that they were even capable, but suddenly, as Mag closed in on my father and his horse, Roi flew past the left side of Heli and we watched as he ran past my father's horse, circled him, and came to stop, in all of his power, in front of Heiður, who simply stopped, throwing Mag from her back, while the deer and the horses quickly moved around him or jumped over his body. Heiður turned immediately and fled back into the forest, leaving Mag lying on the ground face to face with Roi and Pålitlig, who swooped down and mangled Mag's coat with his claws, as he pushed him to the ground.

My mother, who had been holding me pinned to her with her left hand, let out a breath and released her grip on me slightly, but we kept a steady pace along with the three deer, across the land that was slowly becoming desert, leaving Roi to deal with Mag. As I leaned back into the safety of my mother's body, which was warm from the chase, I closed my eyes and wondered at what I had just seen. I thought that I knew what life was. I thought that life was love. That was all I had known until this moment. I thought that life was safe. Danger was what I had just experienced.

Danger. Mag had wanted to harm us. I could see it in his face. There was something in his eyes that I had never seen before. I wouldn't have even called them eyes. Eyes to me were pools of light that I could gaze into and find a soul, but I could not see the soul in Mag's eyes. They were empty. I saw desire— evil desire, force, and power. I saw all these things. I did not see love. I did not know that eyes could be like this. Suddenly, I needed to see my mother's eyes. I opened her veil and stared up at her face, but I could only see the silhouette of her chin, iridescent blue in the light of the moon, and her beautiful neck. I reached up for her as we rode at that great speed toward the desert. Startled a bit, she looked down at me and smiled. Yes, there they were. They were true. But they were eyes too. I looked into them, seeming so mystically blue in the light of the evening, shining out, through the darkness, defeating it. I could gaze into them for hours. She tried to look up again, but I pulled her head back down toward mine. She smiled again, this time seeming to know what I was thinking, what I was looking for. She let me look. If these were eyes, and Mag's were eyes too, then what did that mean of eyes? Could my mother's eyes become like Mag's? Or Mag's like my mother's? I began to understand something more of this world then, though I could not explain it, but I knew that this difference exisited, and somehow, it changed everything.

When we had cleared the rocky land that separated the Ukryty Forest from the Ketidaktahuan Desert, my father paused and turned Keki around to face the area where Roi had overtaken Mag. We all saw Far Larkin's horse run into the forest, and we knew what a formidable force Roi could be, so there was a sense that we could rest for a moment. At that moment that we stopped, we realized that everything had changed. My father and mother dismounted their horses and found each other in the darkness. My mother found her way into my father's arms and I found myself in one of my favorite places, between them. I could feel a certain palpitation in their hearts circulate through mine. It wasn't fear, but it was, I think, a sense of urgency, perhaps mingled with unknowing. Perspiration mixed with the dew in the air, creating a small chill, which the heat of our bodies together dissipated.

The desert looked beautiful. The blueness of the moon fused itself with the white sands, creating what looked like a suspended ocean. Plateaus in the distance gave some concreteness, some sense of a reality where things could be solid and move upward here, but other than that, there was only the sea of sand and a few desert flowers. My father looked out into the distance of the desert, as though looking for something in all the vast expanse of sand. A warm wind came from behind us again, seemingly pushing us into the desert. My father held my mother and I tightly in his arms. We all looked out into the desert together.

Pålitlig came from behind us and rested for a moment on Heli's back. I was glad to see him. So were my mother and father. Had Mag posed a threat to us still, Pålitlig would not have left him. His presence meant that we were safe. We walked over to greet him. He pressed his forehead to my mother's. Rarely did they come this close to each other. There was usually a sense that Pålitlig wished to respect our privacy, but was commissioned, perhaps by the Melekorium, to stay close to us. However, after a battle such as this, it seemed we all needed to reassure each other that we were alive and together. My father rested his hand lightly on Pålitlig's back, a gesture of thanksgiving as I, for the first time, touched the white tuft of downy hair on top of his head as I had always wanted to do. Then I touched my forehead to his and closed my eyes, trying to find the spirit of Pålitlig and share my love with him. For a moment, we looked into each other's eyes and I knew that he knew that I loved him.

Suddenly, his head moved out toward the desert. Food would not have distracted him at this moment. It had to be something more. My mother and father's gaze went out into the desert with Pålitlig's. He alighted from Heli's back and soared up to his eagle's height, and then moved out into the desert winds, which were still moving East, toward Misr. Pålitlig was gone for some time. We did not think that he would us at a time such as this. My parents looked at each other, wondering if there was yet something more important he had to do. Were we safe?

We looked out into the distance, seeing nothing but sand when something in the sky started to make itself seen. After a few moments, it began taking shape. It was long and black, but moved at a great speed, and was coming toward us, like a black cloud, inverted into the shape of a human. As the strange form came closer, we could see that at its top, it had wings. It was Pålitlig! As he flew closer, we could see that he was carrying a long, black piece of cloth in his claws. He dropped the cloth into my father's arms. My mother searched my father's eyes for an answer. They looked back into the forest from which we had come, and out into the desert where Pålitlig had certainly taken this from the head of a Demudi Udi Aramad, one of the sand dwellers who lived in the Ketidaktahuan Desert. But where there was one, there were usually many, and most were not friends of Royameheirs. We did business with them and they with us, but the desert was their land and, though they claimed no rights to any part of it, they respected each tribe's use of certain parts. Anyone travelling through a part of the desert they were using should expect to make their business known. My parents expected this, just not so soon.

  We looked out into the desert for answers, but could find none. What we did find was a form taking shape on the horizon, a great form, which blocked the stars in the sky as it stood upon the crest of a dune in the distance. It paused, perhaps looking at us, as we were looking at it. There was nothing to keep us from being visible to anyone, as we were in a wide open space with the light of the moon illuminating the figures of everything in sight, though they seemed like shadows against the luminescent, glowing sands. My father decided to wait where we were. At least now we were on firm ground and could run quickly if needed. We would wait for the figure to approach, and we knew that it would, since it seemed to be headed directly toward us.

I sensed no fear in my mother's heart as she watched the tall, silent figure approach our family. My father stood in his strength as well. They looked at each other and smiled, held me close. We could tell by this time that it was just one man who came toward us, probably on his way to market in Maisondepahn, though it was really the wrong time of day for even the Demudi Udi Aramad to be travelling. My father looked at the long, black tōb in his hands as the figure approached. It could belong to anyone. The culture of the Demudi Udi Aramad was mysterious to all who lived outside of it and they meant it to remain that way. Very few people were invited into their world who were not born into it. They had their own laws that even government officials would not meddle in, as long as they stayed in the desert, which they usually did. If one of their tribesmen committed an infraction in one of the towns, which they were usually very careful not to do, the tribe would abandon him as though he did not exist. However, if a tribesman went to the law about an infraction committed within the tribe, he and his family could be killed by the tribe. This was their law. They were very serious about their privacy.

It must have been the potential danger posed by the figure that approached mingling with the danger that had just passed, but my mind began to wander toward Far Larkin, just as my mother said to my father, "Stephen, Far."

That was all she needed to say, as she looked into my father's eyes. He just looked at her sympathetically and said, "Yes, Gayle, I know," and then drew us closer to himself. Given the events of the last few hours, we all wondered if our great friend was okay. It would be some time before we knew the answer.

†††

The story of Péttur is one of Far's favorite stories to tell. When Mag took the sword from Péttur's hand, Péttur, though well-armored, sensed that he was on more equal-footing with Far. They both watched as Far's horse and Mag galloped away, and even after the horse had gone into the darkness of the forest, they both stood, watching. Far decided that he would let Péttur make the first move, since he had orders and everything.  He wondered what Péttur was thinking as Mag galloped away and they stood, watching.  He noticed as Péttur's head turned toward his.  He seemed nervous.  Far started to feel sorry for the kid.  He turned, to meet his eyes, but Péttur looked back into the forest, after Mag.

The moment had gone past awkwardness several moments ago, so Far finally said, "Can I get you that water now?"

Péttur shook his head 'yes'.  Far thought that there was more to Péttur than met the untrained eye.  He opened the door and allowed Péttur to enter the Christianson home in front of him.  He offered him the seat where Mag had sat, but he chose the seat next to it instead.  Far poured him a cup of water and sat the cup in front of him as he watched Péttur try to get comfortable sitting in the wooden seat with his metal armor.   Far chuckled to himself, and then remembered that his friends were in harm's way up the road, bringing him back to a place between cautious optimism and thankfulness that he was still standing on two legs.  He decided that there was nothing he could do about his friends just this moment, having no horse, and allowed himself the joy of watching the young soldier slide forward in the chair, stop himself, push himself back into the chair, only to find himself slipping forward again. The trial was to find a position that looked dignified and kept him in the seat, which was the challenge. He finally settled for staying in the seat, but sat low in the chair and ended up looking like a little child, which Far kind of liked.

Far sat in the seat where Mag had sat, at the corner of the table that sat him adjacent to Péttur. He looked at Péttur and couldn't help but to smirk a bit.

"What?" Péttur asked him.

"May I ask your name?" Far said, gently.

"I thought it was your custom not to ask guests for their names for three days." Péttur said nervously.

"It is, but you are going to break my legs. I guess that means that I'm your guest in a way, and in our culture guests have the right to know the name of their host," Far casually remarked, then smiled, mainly with his eyes.

Péttur looked away from Far. He was thinking. He liked to see Péttur think. "Then what is your name?" Péttur asked suddenly, letting Far know that he was the host and did not intend to break Far's legs.

"My name is Far Larkin. Pleased to meet you, uh..." he said as he held out his hand for Péttur to take.

"Péttur," he said. "My name is Péttur," and left Far's hand suspended in the air over the table.

"That's an unusual name for a Kiläl," Far said, as he took a drink of water.

"I wasn't born Kiläl," Péttur offered.

"You converted," Far supposed.

"Something like that," Péttur shrugged, looking into his empty glass.

"May I offer you another drink?" Far asked. Péttur offered him his glass. As Far walked over to the sink to draw the water, he tried to make sense of Péttur's name and his features. There was something about him that he recognized.

"May I ask your father's name?" Far asked, as he sat down at the table.

"My father's name is Jonathan," Péttur said, looking away, into the night.

"His last name?" Far asked.

"McGovern," ," Péttur said, resignedly.

"He is a soldier," Far stated, matter-of-factly.

"Yes, he is a soldier; a Royameheir," ," Péttur stated, looking at Far.

"A brave soldier," Far stated.

"That is what I've heard, yes," Péttur stated with some pride and some resentment.

"I was with him in the battle of Lys," Far stated, sensing that Péttur was perhaps unaware of who his father was.

"So was I," Péttur stated, beckoning Far to ask him how.

"You were there?" Far asked.

"Yes, I was there." Péttur stated, looking into Far's eyes with his green eyes.

Far searched his mind to see if he could remember seeing Péttur during the battle. Things that happen in battle are so often seared amazingly into the memory, but of course many things are not noticed because of the personal intensity of the battle. "Do you know what happened to him at that battle?" Far asked as sensitively as possible.

"I do," Péttur stated.

"He was killed by a Kiläl soldier," Far stated, beckoning Péttur to come into the light.

"I know," Péttur said, looking away. It seemed a tear was forming, but he drew it back and composed himself.

"And still you fight for them?" Far asked.

"Yes," Péttur said, raising his voice. "Still I fight for them. I have no choice. I've made my choices. My father made his and I made mine and what I wanted to happen happened on that battlefield and I helped it and it is done,"

Péttur said as a single tear fell from his eye. "It is done," he repeated.

"Nothing is done, Péttur," Far said.

"It is done and there is nothing I can do about it now," Péttur said. "I wanted him to die and now he is dead."

"Did he do something to you?" Far asked.

"You Royameheirs. You act like you are all so perfect. My father was anything but perfect," Péttur said. "You're not perfect. You are worse than the Kiläl. At least the Kiläl don't pretend to be perfect. I know that they lie and they cheat and they steal, just like you. Only they admit it. They don't pretend that they are something they are not."

"No, Péttur. We are not perfect, but we try to be, just like everyone else. And we encourage others to try, but we are human. We are not perfect. But we seek the help of the Royame here and in the world to come for help. That is all," Far explained.

"Even you?" Péttur sneered. "You walk around in your uniform with those emblems."

"Yes, Péttur, even me," Far said, "What did your father do to you?" Far asked.

"He controlled my life," Péttur said. "Every second of it."

"I see," Far said, realizing that he was dealing with a normal phase of life, which had grown into something extraordinarily harmful, given the young man's capabilities. But why had this happened? He wondered. He knew many young Royameheirs whose fathers were soldiers and they had not become Kiläl soldiers.

"I had no choice," said Péttur, "He said I had to be a soldier, so I'm a soldier." Péttur tried again to relax, but still could not find a way to get comfortable in his armor.

"A Kiläl soldier," Far corrected. "Would you like to take some of your armor off?" Far suggested. "It looks a bit uncomfortable."

Péttur thought about it for a few moments. Far watched as his blue eyes searched the room for an answer. Far desired greatly that Péttur would do it, knowing that if the armor came off, it would be a step toward finding the true Péttur again. Péttur looked at Far, searching hesitantly for an answer there.

"No, thank you," Péttur decided, straightening himself up, trying to look more comfortable.

"At least the helmet. I'm no threat to you," Far said.

Péttur smirked under his breath as he looked at Far and said, "I wonder," and removed his helmet, revealing the same milky blonde curls that Far remembered his father having had. His mind drifted back to the day on the battlefield when he was standing underneath the willow tree, scanning the battlefield for soldiers he could render aid to. The confusion of violence and the adrenalin rushing through his body left him standing motionless for some time, watching soldiers from both sides fall immediately dead or slightly wounded, both situations being ones in which he could offer no help, unless they were Royameheir, in which case, he would help to prepare their bodies for burial after the fighting had ended.

He kept scanning the battlefied, trying to understand what was happening, keeping his mind clear in the midst of the confusion of the battle. He watched as John McGovern approached a Kiläl soldier with his sword drawn. He did everything as the Royameheirs are taught to do. He offered the Kiläl soldier his life and asked him to depart from the battle in peace, in answer to which the Kiläl soldier lunged at him, striking his arm plate.

Far tried to watch the other scenes on the battlefield and later thought that perhaps it was the shock of white hair and the fairness of John's skin juxtaposed against the dark, fully-armored Kiläl soldier that kept drawing his eye back to that particular scene, for there were many that were happening. He was looking at John McGovern at the moment that he, uncharacteristically, stopped fighting altogether and the Kiläl soldier struck the fatal blow that would take the life of Péttur's father. The soldier struck him in the neck and left him for dead, but he was still alive when Far reached his side.

He remembered being there before he thought of being there. He could not remember, he realized as he sat himself down beside John, holding his head in his hand, how he had gotten there. He could not think of whether to apply the holy oil that he carried with him to John's body – his hands and his feet, his forehead, or to wait for him to speak.

He asked him if he would like to confess anything. "My son." The only two words he was able to get out. He wanted to say more, but was unable. Far told him that it was enough. God understood his sorrow. He prayed the prayers over him that would remove the stain of sin from his soul and reconcile him with God before he left the world. He applied the sacred oil to his hands and feet, and held his head in his hand, waiting for the last breath.

He had laid John's head on the ground and watched as the red of the blood from the wound in his neck streamed into his white hair, noting in the poetic reflection of the white and the red mingling together, the purity of the Royameheir and his martyrdom. He wondered at this soldier who had just reminded him of the battle of dark with light as he had stood across from the Kiläl, and sacrificed himself. It was just as he was coming to his senses, and remembering that he was on a battle ground, that he was suddenly lifted up into the air by Gezur and found himself on the horse, thinking that his life too was about to come to an end until Stephen Christianson, another blonde-haired soldier, suddenly saved him. A coincidence?

As he sat across from Péttur, Far's heart seemed to be unable to tell the difference between the soldier who had risked his life on behalf of the Royame on the battlefield and the young, confused Royameheir dressed as a Kiläl soldier in front of him. He thought that it was Péttur's hair, so much like his father's. Something is his heart told Far to push the issue with Péttur.

"How long have you been a Kiläl soldier, Péttur?" Far asked nonchalantly.

"Since my father told me to get out of the house – since I was eighteen, " Péttur offered.

"That must have been difficult – to be on your own like that at such a young age," Far offered.

"I don't know. Just life, I guess," Péttur answered, seeming to feel somewhat more comfortable with Far.

For some reason, the thought that Péttur was at the Battle of Lys kept persisting in his mind. Something told him that going down this road would be difficult, but he felt that he had to do it for some reason. A shot like lightning ran up his spine as he asked, "So you have seen battle then."

"Of course I have," Péttur said, feeling confident in his abilities as a soldier and showing it in his posture as he sat up straighter and moved his chest outward a bit.

"Do you like it?" Far asked.

"It's in the blood, I guess," Péttur said as he sat back, trying to shrink away from something. It was that something that Far sensed he needed to understand.

"I wonder how it is in your blood to kill Royameheirs, Péttur."

"I wonder how it is in the blood of Royameheirs to kill Kiläl," Péttur countered. "Protectors of life," he scoffed.

"Only in self-defense, Péttur," Far reminded him.

"Not always," Péttur defended himself.

"You're right. Not always, but as a policy. We try," Far offered. "I am sorry if we have failed, but we do try, Péttur."

Péttur looked out into the dark world through the window. He seemed to be weighing this. "So that's the difference between my father and me," Péttur asked.

"Well, the main difference now is that you are alive and he is not," Far offered, "perhaps it was once a difference."

"My father will go to heaven for what he did to me and I will go to hell," Péttur decided.

"Not necessarily," Far said in the most consoling way he could. "That is for God to judge," Far said.

"No. I know," Péttur said. "It doesn't matter anymore," he shrugged, though he was seeming to become agitated. His leg began to move as he fidgeted with the glass in front of him. Far could see that there was a battle taking place. He would expect it. Once a Royameheir, always a Royameheir. His conscience had been formed in truth and it would continue to call him back to truth until he arrived there, no matter how long it would take.

"Nothing is set in stone, Péttur. There is no mistake that cannot be made right so long as you are alive." Far saw his chance and took it. He called Péttur back into the light of truth.

"Some sins can't be forgiven," Péttur said.

"That's not true, Péttur," Far offered. You are saying that there is something that God cannot do, that you are greater, that your sin is greater than his mercy. That is just not true," Far offered, moving instinctively closer to Péttur.

As Far moved toward him, Péttur sprung from the chair and moved backwards so that his back was to a wall. "You don't know me," Péttur shouted at Far. Far saw that he had struck a nerve, but his fatherly instincts told him to move into the wound, now that it was open. He knew that these wounds sometimes never re-opened once they shut and, like any wound, if he left it alone, it would scab, with the pain locked almost invisibly inside, perhaps forever.

"You're right, Péttur, I don't know you very well yet, but I knew your father," Far offered by way of consolation, "and he was a good man. You are good. Your family is good. Your blood is good," Far said, as he stood and moved gently toward Péttur. Péttur moved his hand to a dagger nestled in the armor next to his left hipbone. "Don't come any closer," he warned.

"I'm not going to hurt you, Péttur." Far pleaded. "I know that you are good, Péttur."

"No!" Péttur yelled as he took the long, heavy dagger from its scabbard. "You don't know anything! You don't know me! I killed him," Péttur sobbed, as he tried to strengthen his hold on the heavy dagger made of Eiwengaard steel, but the strength tried to leave his body as the emotion of the past surged into the present. Far had been down this road before, but never with someone holding a knife. It made this intense situation, he noted, that much more intense.

"Who did you kill?" Far asked, knowing the answer.

"You know who," Péttur sobbed, still trying to keep control of the long dagger in front of him.  Far's  heart wept for Péttur.  He suddenly remembered where he had seen Péttur's helmet.  He was the Kiläl whose form was burned into Far's mind in the fight of John McGovern and the Kiläl soldier— one seemingly a son of darkness, the other of light – a father and a son, he now realized. 'If only he knew how much I care for him,' Far wished to himself.  The scene of the young, regretful man before him holding the dagger seemed like the physical manifestation of situations he had been in many times before. 'How many people wielded metaphorical daggers?' Far wondered to himself, 'killing each other so that people wouldn't see the darkness within themselves.  How many killed their fathers or their mothers with words or gestures?'

"It's not as unusual as you think, Péttur," Far offered. "We kill people in our minds or with our words all the time. I was actually just thinking that this real knife you have pointed at me here is almost a relief compared to the invisible ones I deal with all the time." Far tried to force a smile, noticing that Péttur's grip on the blade seemed to be loosening.

Far took a step toward Péttur. "You don't have to punish yourself, son. Wouldn't you like to see your mother again?" Far asked. It was the wrong question.

"My mother?" Péttur yelled through renewed sobs at Far as the strength returned with the unearthed anger unleashed with the thought of his mother. "How can I face my mother?" Péttur shouted at Far as though it was his fault. Far was used to it. Unphased, he pressed on. "She loves you, Péttur," he insisted. "Stop it!" Péttur yelled. Far tried to speak again, but Péttur yelled, "Stop it! Shut up!" as he lunged forward and moved the blade to Far's throat. Far's knees almost buckled beneath him, but he righted himself as he found Péttur's eyes and held his gaze.

"I have my orders for you!" Péttur reminded Far.

"Calm down, Péttur," Far lightly demanded.

"No. I tell you what to do," Péttur insisted as he moved the point of the blade into Far's throat, causing him to cough slightly while trying to keep from piercing his own throat with the blade.

"Don't make the same mistake twice, Péttur. Forgive yourself. Don't add me to the list of things you regret. We can talk about this," Far insisted. "This pain can be over. Just put the knife down. Stop."

"I am Kiläl," Péttur said. "I am a Kiläl soldier, a warrior," Péttur reminded himself, trying to talk himself out of the guilt he felt over his father's death.

"You are Royameheir," Far insisted, searching for Péttur's eyes. Oftentimes the brink of light was at the edge of darkness. He reached for the light that he knew still burned inside Péttur, the enlightenment instilled in him by his baptism into the Royame when he was a baby.

"No! I'm Kiläl!" Péttur shouted as he struck Far's left knee with the heavily-weighted end of the Eiwengaard dagger, forcing him to the ground in a pool of pain. Far stifled the cry that tried to come from his mouth. His knee was broken. Through the heaving of his breath, he lifted his hand to Péttur and said, "Péttur, no. Please. No more." But Péttur was intent now on carrying out Mag's orders. Before he knew what happened, Far felt the blow to his right knee in a flash of Péttur's heavily-armored leg coming down to crush his bone before he suddenly lost consciousness from the sudden pain.

†††

Somewhere in the darkness, Far thought he could hear the sobs of a boy and felt soft, wet drops on his forehead, then the sound of heavy armor that had lost the strength to carry itself scraping slowly across the floor. From the darkness in the back of his mind, he waited for the reassurance of the sound of a closing door, signaling that he was safe.  Some part of his mind that was responsible for awareness and safety waited, and waited, and waited.  He wanted to call out to Péttur, sensing that he was still there, but unable to reach him from the blackness.  He heard sobs and the words, "I'm sorry" repeated over and over again coming from the direction of the door.  His saçerdōtan senses still called out to the lost son from within, hearing his sorrow, but he could not rouse himself back into consciousness.  His heart went through the process of forgiving Péttur, crying out within for the pain of this lost son of the Royame. In his mind, his arm reached out, though he knew that it remained limply by his side.

His protetive senses, as they were able, listened for what was next.  His ears roused and tried to communicate to his brain through the pain-unconsciousness—The sound of a wooden door closing gently, but firmly, that registered somewhere in the blackened waves.  Then the blackness overtook him.

†††

It was the middle of the night and the air was mostly warm as we watched the dark figure on the moon-lit horizon make its way steadily toward us, moving up and down with the gate of what would soon become one of my favorite animals – a camel. The figure was taller to me than anything I had seen before, though it was far off. It reminded me, from where I lay watchfully in my mother's arms, like a tree moving its long, hardened roots, gangling toward us. It confused me, but my mother's heart kept its steady, smooth beat. My parents trusted in the Royame, she would later tell me, and she and my father knew that help from beyond our world would be sent for us in the form of humans along our way. They trusted that this was what the looming figure represented, but my heart was still charged with the dangerous scene I had just witnessed and listened for the slightest change in my mother's body that would indicate danger.

Deep within, I longed for the presence of Far Larkin and searched my heart for him and his protection, as the scene of the mad man re-surfaced in my mind— his evil eyes riding the back of Heiður. This sight had shocked me and confused me.  As I lay wishing for my spiritual father, it was the first time that the sign of the Lark came to me to comfort and reassure me in a time of distress. My heart was always united with Far's and, even so far away, Far's saçerdōtan senses knew somehow that I needed him. I heard, from where I cannot imagine, the sound of a lark singing, uncharacteristically, in the dark night, and then a cool breeze came and tickled me, especially on my forehead where I always loved to share the greeting of the Royame with Far, just as had happened before we departed Hyamæa, and suddenly my heart knew that all was well.

†††

As Far lay unconscious on the floor of Hyamæa, he found himself, in his mind, back in the cathedral where the hands were laid upon him that conferred upon him the powers of the saçerdōtum.  He found himself once again standing in the semi-circular line of men, now kneeling, who had endured the grueling training required of those wanting to enter the saçerdōtum. They surrounded the bishop and other saçèrdōtés, listening intently as the prayers were prayed over them by the man who had the power to confer upon men the powers of the Royame.  He remembered the thought that kept recurring as he listened to the words—'This is it. Turn around forever or stay forever. This is it. Turn around. Walk away. This cannot be meant for you. You are just a man'. He heard the words, "No one here present for the purpose of taking orders shall come forward to be ordained under any pretext, if he be irregular, excommunicated by law,...

The bishop applied the sacred oil to his hands, but instead of the small amount that was usually rubbed on the body by the thumb, the bishop took a paint brush and continued to anoint his left hand over and over again with the oil that soaked the brush. He wanted to tell the bishop that this was not the correct form, but he didn't want to embarrass him, especially with so many people present, but his desire to follow the form correctly awoke within him a feeling of anxiety as he tried to remove his hand from the bishop's reach, but couldn't. The anxiety increased until he awoke from his sleep to find Heiður licking his palm.

His relief at seeing his trusted horse was enough to make him forget the pain in his legs at first. He held on to the floor as the pain surged through his body in waves while his mind tried to remember where he was and what had happened. He was alive. This was good, he decided, though it was terribly painful to be alive and unable to walk. He looked around the room. He was alone, obviously. That was good. The door and the window were broken. He remembered the sound of the door shutting. It was the last sound he had heard. Heiður rubbed his nose against the side of Far's face, trying to nudge him back into reality. He saw the blood on Heiður's nose where he had broken the window with it. Far rubbed it gently, wondering at the love of this animal, and thankful for it. Heiður must have broken through the door when he couldn't get through the window, Far thought. Had he ever heard of an animal doing such a thing? He couldn't remember if he had. Other, curious animals had gathered around Hyamæa to see what was happening, but remained outside of the house. He was glad to see them. He felt less alone.

His mind started to try to understand the next step. He looked at Heiður and said, "Well, old boy, I guess we are going to have to get home. He stopped for a moment to reflect on the events of the evening. Where was Mag? Péttur had obviously fled. Mag was riding his horse. If Heiður was here, then perhaps Mag had not been able to reach the family. He searched his heart for the truth of what had happened to them, asking God to reveal to him in prayer the truth, even if the truth was hard. He closed his eyes and searched his heart for the answer. Suddenly a smile swept over his face as he found the family in his heart, though he hoped they were far, far away. He knew they were safe, for now at least.

†††

Mag was confused by the behavior of the lion as he sat, defeated, in the moonlit sand with Roi lying across from him, seemingly becoming tired. "Well, even a lion has to sleep, I imagine," he said out loud. Roi had paced in front of Mag for over an hour, lunging at him if he tried to escape back into the forest, where he wished to flee. The desert without supplies or transportation was not an option, even if it was where his duty lie. It would be futile to try to attempt it. He would have to go back to the house, get provisions, and then set out again, if he could get away from this lion. 'Why won't it attack me?' He wondered to himself.

Roi would not attack Mag. No animals who lived in Hyamæa would harm a human being purposefully, without being attacked. The transformation that took place in the hearts of Hyamæa included the hearts of animals. Mag was lucky.

"This lion will have to sleep or eat, one or the other," Mag thought to himself, as the thought of sleep began to take over his own thoughts as well. He felt himself growing tired as the weariness from the chase and the travel from Maisondepahn began to take the place of the adrenalin that had been rushing through his veins, which now waned since the lion seemed, for some reason, to be only a guard and not a predator.

'Well, if he is my guard, he can guard my sleeping body,' thought Mag as he removed his black coat and rolled it into a pillow. 'And if he decides to eat me, I would rather be asleep anyway.' As he lay on the ground, he heard the sound of something moving behind him. He decided to ignore it, as there would surely be all sorts of things moving around out here, but the sound seemed to want his attention. Finally, he looked behind him and saw the crow he had called out of the forest.

"Still here?" he asked. "Well, aren't you loyal," he half-sneered. The crow sought the relationship with Mag, which had brought him out of his old hum-drum life and into this new life of purpose and excitement – the tool of a human being. He stayed close to Mag, waiting to be called back into action.

"You want something to do, do you?" Mag said to him. "Well, go find the boy and bring him here."

The crow alighted into the air and turned back toward the forest.

## Chapter 5

### Winds of Protection

Péttur had been traveling through the forest as quickly as his legs could carry him toward the boat that had brought him and Mag to Hyamæa. When he would tell the story to people later, he would recall that the only thought that he had as he was traveling away from Hyamæa was to find his mother and make things right with her. The tears for what he had just done to the saçèrdōté who had tried to reach out to him and the tears for his father mingled and brought forth a storm in the soul of the young soldier, who now looked like a scared child, traveling alone through an unknown land, not caring where he was going— just going fast, away, though he seemed to barely be able to get the Eiwengaarde armor off the ground because of the heaviness in his heart. He wanted nothing more of being a soldier – any kind of soldier. He was done with it. It was his father's idea for him anyway and he had never wanted to be a soldier. As a child, he had remembered as he was sitting across from Far, he had wanted to be, of all things, a saçèrdōté, but his father only mocked him when he expressed this desire. "We are soldiers," he had told Péttur, "and you must not fight it. You must be smart to be a saçèrdōté. It takes much school and we have not the blood for it or the brains," he had said, half-laughing as he pulled Péttur to himself and rubbed his white curls hard, like soldiers do to each other.

"But saçèrdōtés *are* warriors, Papa," Péttur had said to him. It all came flooding back with the tears. He remembered the desires of his childhood and the beautiful lady who had come to him in a dream and placed her hand on his heart, claiming it for herself. He had always kept it for her. He had tried to date like the other boys, but in his heart he could never find a piece of it to give away to another. It was claimed by her and he could feel her with him until the day he slew his father. When that left, when she left, he gave up on life altogether and decided to do as much damage to himself and others as he could since his life was over anyway without her, without a father or a mother.

As he remembered his desire to be a saçèrdōté, he stopped and looked up into the full moon. He remembered her, the beautiful lady. She was real, from the place beyond this world, he knew, that was real. He had always known it for some reason, even if others didn't. They questioned, but he knew. As memories of his desires and the lady came back to him, he fell to his knees. He begged forgiveness for everything he had done.

Thunder sounded within his body as memories of his actions flooded to the forefront of his mind. Tears came from without and within, it seemed, seemingly jumping from his eyes as he remembered and felt sorrow for the moment he killed his father. Convulsions racked his body, which was encumbered by the metal of his Kiläl armor, which he could now feel pushing against every part of his skin. He tore the metal from his body, bloodying his hands with a vest that would not come off fast enough. He unfastened the armor on his legs and threw it as far as he could, listening with satisfaction if it hit a tree or a rock, damaged beyond repair, he hoped. He felt free, but vulnerable as he sat on the dirt road in the black silks that he wore under his armor. He felt the cool wind on his body and welcomed it.

He knew that a stone thrown the right way could now kill him, but he didn't care. He took deep breaths and now, with the armor off his body, felt that he could fly. He rose up to his knees, thinking he would move on, but with the armor off and his body free, as he drew breath in, memories rose anew in his mind. He sat motionless and then bent his head over his knees as the memories came flooding back.

He remembered the moment he left home, determined that he would do as his father willed, but he would be a Kiläl soldier, not a Royameheir. Nothing would hurt his father more than his son becoming what he hated most. The ultimate rebellion. Then his mind wandered to places it had not been in years. He saw his father lifting him up onto his shoulders and running with him through the woods. Each picture was like a small dagger, piercing his heart, causing salty tears to stream down his face. He saw his great hand holding his small face when he was just a boy. How he thought a hand could never be so large. He looked then, through his tears, at his own hands. He saw how they had grown, but never to the size of his father's.

Every loving touch his father had given him seemed to flood into his soul. He looked again at his hands. "How could I have used these hands to kill the man who created them?" he wondered as sobs came anew to his body, throwing him forward, his forehead pressed hard against the ground. The tears fell into the ground, creating a paste of dirt and tears. He pushed his forehead into the cool earth, wishing to go down, down, down into the dirt, wishing to join his father, wondering how he could live. His fists grabbed the earth, the grass, anything that made him feel like he was not spinning out of control. He pounded the earth, as he tried to beat this reality out of it or give back to this life what it had given him.

Then he reminded himself that he had done this. These were all his own choices... to become a Kiläl soldier, to kill his own father, to rebel, and he was determined to become nothing because that was what he was, and to tell everyone what had happened and be shunned by everyone. Perhaps that would stall the pain somehow. To suffer for what he had done. This thought brought him some peace and so he stayed there, allowing the thoughts to subside. Once he had an action, it seemed to calm him.

Then he felt the fatigue of his spent energy, and he laid on his back and looked up at the sky, seemingly, he thought, for the first time. He noticed the way the moonlight played off of the green leaves, and saw the stars twinkling between them. Then, just as he was feeling himself drift into a sleep the likes of which he had not felt since he was a boy, from somewhere he knew not, but sensed that it must be from the world beyond, he felt – love. Love for himself. He knew it could not be his own love because he knew he had no love left for himself.

Now it was Far's eyes he saw as his mind began to collapse into the darkness. He heard his words now. Far – another father whom he had tried to slay. He saw the smile in Far's eyes, even as he admitted his murder, forgiving him. He remembered everything Far had said in the house, how he had offered him food and rest and, above all, love. He could see all the things he had been trying to not see.

A single tear fell down his cheek. Just as he was about to judge himself irredeemable, he heard Far say, "Everyone kills in one way or another." Sobs came anew to his body. The sounds came from someplace within him that he didn't recognize as the tears leapt from his eyes. He looked up into the trees. The moonlight sliding through the branches seemed to bathe him in new light. The light seemed new somehow, like he had never seen light before. Pain and joy mingled within his heart and he breathed a breath that felt like a new breath. He stood within his truth, somehow strong enough to hold it all – even his father's death. He held it, but felt that he was not holding it alone. As he looked up toward the moon, he could feel the presence of the lady again in his heart. It was too much to bear. She was here in the midst of all this? She could see him, how weak he was, how awful he had been. He wanted to hide from her, but the more shame he felt, the more he felt her penetrating his heart with love. He could feel her love for him mixing with all of the sorrow. He could feel her existence. She was telling him that he had been heard – and forgiven.

He searched his mind and remembered that this could happen. The sacrament of healing was not bound to the earth. He heard one of his childhood teachers saying it. It could come from above, from God, because ultimately, it always did come from above. He had been heard. His sorrow was real and it was heard in the Royame. Tears continued to flow down his face as memories came to the surface, revealing Truth after Truth to him. He could feel her presence in his heart again for the first time in years – she who he thought was gone, she who he thought had left him. No words could describe his joy. But it was he who had left her. He knew it from the bottom of his soul. He sat up and looked up into the moon, which seemed somehow to be a reflection of her beauty. He wanted to touch it. It was blue and luminescent, like her face the night he saw her. It reminded him so much of her and he could feel her love course through his heart, bringing it back to life. He would do anything to stay with her. He knew that he would have to listen, that it would be hard, but he didn't care. He searched his heart for a purpose. His longing to share all of this with someone led him directly to one man. He knew exactly what he had to do. He had to return to the house. Suddenly, his love for Far Larkin, the saçèrdōté who had fought for his soul, came into his mind. He knew what he had to do next. He had to make sure that Far was okay.

    He pulled himself up from the ground and began to walk back toward the house. He felt so light without the Kiläl armor and, freed from the weight of the lies he had carried, he started to jog, and then suddenly he was flying on his feet toward the house, finding energy from somewhere beyond him, it seemed. He felt that he could run forever and never tire. And for the first time that he could remember since he had left home those years ago, he was smiling. Once in a while, a tear fell from his eye, rode the wind, and landed on the ground behind him like a tiny, beautiful, moon-lit diamond.

†††

Far pulled himself, with the help of Heiður's rein, up onto the kitchen chair where he had sat not too long ago with Péttur. He poured himself a glass of water from the pitcher that still sat on the table from their earlier discussion. Heiður came and nuzzled his nose into the pitcher and began to drink. He tried to anyway. Far looked longingly at the faucet, only feet away, but it could have been a mile, wishing that he could turn it on for Heiður. He tilted the pitcher so that Heiður's pink tongue could take some of the water. He drank some himself, feeling better as the soothing water flowed into his body— a remembrance of life in place of what had seemed like the beginning of death not long ago. It didn't seem that his wounds were fatal though, only extremely painful for now. He offered the pain up for the family that was traveling through the desert, hopefully, by now, and decided not to prolong the inevitable any longer. He would have to mount Heiður. There was no getting around it. This was going to hurt, but just for a moment, he reminded himself, and then he would be atop the steed and on his way back to Maisondepahn. Maisondepahn, he thought to himself. What comfort that word had brought only days ago. But he would return to the suffering of his people.

He pulled himself up onto the top of the kitchen table with his arms and brought Heiður close to the table, grabbed his left leg with his arm and vaulted himself up onto the horse using his lame right leg, which screamed in pain while his lungs expelled a quick, deep breath as he barely hung onto Heiður's neck with his arms. The thought of having to do it over again was enough to make him hold on tight. He pushed himself up into place and was finally atop Heiður. As he could not properly place his legs in the stirrups or use his legs to hang on, he took a leather rein from his satchel, pressed his legs against the saddle and secured them with the leather. He bent down to finish what water was left in the pitcher, guided Heiður over to the faucet, took his water skins out of the saddle bags and filled them, took some crackers and a few pieces of dried meat from the cabinets, and proceeded to walk, miraculously, out of Hyamæa.

As Heiður walked out of the house, he noticed that the full moon was heading down toward the horizon, but was still lighting the night sky. The whites of eyes, both large and small, were scattered throughout the trees, carefully watching him and Heiður, as they prepared to leave.

The presence of the animals of Hyamæa was reassuring, as he knew that he was the only human around, at least for now. He looked toward the stables, wondering if he had enough time to feed Heiður. Surely there would be something to eat along the way, he thought. Taking the mountain pass, he knew that there would be places where Heiður could eat. He looked left toward the desert, the way the family had traveled. He wished he was able to follow. He looked right toward the ocean— a quicker route to Maisondepahn, but he would have to leave Heiður behind once he reached the boat. He couldn't do that.

He looked ahead to the trail that was forest for a few miles and then quickly rose into the mountains and to the pass that traveled over Mt. Baekdu and Mt. Langya Anhui, then down to the plains of Njardovik that lay on the edge of Maisondepahn.

How he longed to see those plains. He looked left and right, then headed into the forest, picturing home in his mind and the loving people who would tend to his wounds. He smiled as he thought about the women fighting over whose home he would stay in and whose food he would eat first. That would be all the motivation he would need to make it all the way home. He looked at the leaves that seemed to glow blue in the moonlight and then fade to blackness, as they flowed deep into the woods, and knew that was his path.

†††

My father and I were playing the game we like to play where we look into each other eyes and laugh, when suddenly his eyes turned from mine and up to the figure that had approached enough to reveal the features of his face. Pålitlig had been circling around the figure to let him know that he was being carefully watched, but as my father's demeanor toward the traveler was made known in his smile and the twinkling of his eyes, Pålitlig came to rest on my father's saddle, facing the stranger.

"Gercek!" My father laughed, and walked up to greet the traveler on the camel. "Of all the people who would be traveling through the desert tonight."

"What do you mean, Stephen? I am coming at the time and place you appointed for us two weeks ago this night." Gercek recalled matter-of-factly for my father as he dismounted his camel and embraced my father.

My father stared at him and then looked to my mother. "I haven't left Hyamæa in over a year, Gercek, and I myself did not know that I would be traveling tonight, dear friend."

"Well, your Royame is a mystery, as you have said and I have seen that this is to be the case. And your animals share that life, I see," he said looking at Pålitlig. "You really should have warned me in the vision, Stephen, about the eagle that would swoop down toward my face and grab my tōb from my head. Next time you come to me without realizing it, Stephen, please warn me about such things so that I may be prepared," he laughed, looking at Pålitlig's claws. "Have you seen those claws up close, Stephen? They're really something when they are one finger's length from your eyeball. You really must warn me next time."

"But then you might not come, my friend," my father smiled back at him.

"The mystical life I lived in the desert has only deepened since you baptized me into the life of the Royame. If it was not you who told me to meet you here, I need no answers. It is enough for me that you are here and I am here. And this must be Grace," he said as he looked at me, smiling. "May I?" he asked my father, as he bent down and motioned that he would like to give me the greeting of the Royame. My father nodded 'yes' and this man with the velvety brown skin, large, black eyebrows, that matched his curly, black hair, and white, smiling teeth, bent down and touched his forehead to mine. It seemed for a moment that the sun rose in my mind when he touched his forehead to mine. I giggled and smiled and lifted my hand up to touch his face.

"She is something wonderful, isn't she?" he said to my father and then turned to my mother. A tear came to his eye as he looked upon her and knelt down and took her hand in his. "My lady," he said, "as his forehead bent to her hand," it is my greatest honor to meet you at last." My mother motioned for him to stand.

"Gercek," she said, and smiled into his eyes as they looked at each other, knowing so much about each other, but having never yet met. "I have waited for this moment for some time," she said. "If not for you, perhaps Stephen and I never would have..." He stopped her. "No, my lady. You know that if it had not been me, L'Agneau would have found another way."

"But he didn't, Gercek," my mother continued, "he found you and you found Stephen and Stephen and I found each other. We owe you our lives."

"The debt, as you know, has already been repaid, my lady, and now it is I who am forever in the debt of you and your family. How does one repay eternal life? There is no end to the debt I owe you in this world, but let us not waste any time. The desert will become a hot place soon. If we leave now, we will make it to my camp before the sun reaches the center of the sky. Let us go."

My father looked back to the place where Mag went down.

"What is it, Stephen?" Gercek asked.

"Probably nothing. One of the king's men was chasing us. We lost him a few miles back and he's well-guarded, but Roi, the lion who is guarding him, is of our home and won't harm a human. He will have to leave to eat at some point, I think, and the man will be released."

"Then let us not waste time. Mount your horses," Gercek said.

My mother mounted Heli and my father handed me up into her arms, then mounted his own horse as Gercek took his place atop his camel, Vărsi. Gercek, who was facing the desert, turned and looked at my father with a smile I had already fallen in love with. His smile broadened and his eyes twinkled in the moonlight as he said to my father, "How fast do you travel, Stephen?"

"As fast as your camel will go, I imagine," my father answered.

"Oh? Gercek asked, as his smile grew even larger. "Did you know that camels can fly?"

"No," My father laughed as he threw Gercek's tōb to him and looked at my mother.

"Yes. This is not sand. It is air. And these are not legs. These are wings!" he laughed as he folded the tōb expertly around the top of his head.

"Okay." My father laughed. "Let us see then."

"Okay. Hold on tight!" He cried as he gave Vărsi a few taps on each of his sides, bent down into the wind, and, as he promised, flew across the sand."

"I clung to the black gauze of my mother's veil and pressed my face into her belly as I felt her strong arm pulling me into herself as Heli began to gallop and then that thing happened that happened before. I knew that we were moving fast, but it felt like a gentle rocking back and forth as we glided across the desert, and then, secure in the safety of our new- found friend, I fell asleep.

✝✝✝

Just as Far was getting ready to move onto the trail, he looked down at Heiður and saw that he had been through a trial. He seemed tired. "Have you slept, old boy? I got a little sleep back there, but you. You haven't slept in days, have you? Let me get you some oats. I know there is some good food here."

With that, Far walked Heiður over to the stables and found him some oats to eat. Sensing the urgency of the situation, he refused to eat at first, but after a few moments, resignedly bent his head down and then began devouring the oats and sweet barley that were left in the trough. Far took a moment to pray.

He closed his eyes and tried to focus on his heart. He prayed for Mag and for all of his enemies. He tried to feel love inside his heart for him. He knew that any bitterness toward anyone would lead to coldness and that meant death— a living death. When he could feel his desire for Mag's change of heart and his well-being, his mind went to Péttur. It was still not hard to find love for the young man. Far smiled a little when he thought of him standing against the wall in that Kiläl suit— a young Royameheir who should have been in school or fighting in the army of the Royame, but there he was, the ultimate defiance. He was a strong one, Far thought to himself. If he ever returns...

At that moment, Far heard something moving behind him. 'Mag,' he thought to himself. 'I should have fled.' He moved all of Heiður's body into the stable, hoping that he could shield them from sight, though he was sure that they would be found. He prayed that if this was the time of his death, that his soul be cleansed and prepared. Heiður tried to move back against the stable, feeling stifled by the lack of movement. Far tried to stop him.

He listened as footsteps ran to the door of Hyamæa and opened them. He could hear the person calling for someone. It sounded like a young man. He called a name again. It sounded like his name. The door opened again. "Far!" The voice cried. He didn't recognize it. It sounded like a boy. "Far!" the voice sobbed. "No. Where are you?" "Where are you?"

Far turned his body around so that he could see out of the stable door. He saw a young man in black holding his head in a mound of white curls, sitting defeated as a child on the front steps of Hyamæa. 'Péttur?' he thought. But it couldn't be. The figure seemed harmless, whoever it was. He stepped with Heiður gently out into the night air and looked at the person who was too lost in his suffering to notice that Heiður had walked directly up to him and pushed his nose into his hand.

He looked up and the expression of joy on his face, Far recalled later, he had never seen the likes of before. He put his hands to Far's knee and wept over it as he laid his forehead against it and sobbed, "I'm sorry. I'm so sorry."

"I know," Far said as he put his hand on Péttur's head. He did know. He had seen this miracle of grace a thousand times before and each time, it astounded him. Each time was like the first time because it came to no two people alike. He would have gladly given his knees to see this, or even his life. "I know, son."

Péttur looked up at Far and saw the forgiveness in his eyes that he had felt as he lay on the forest floor. It was real, he knew. It was really real and somehow it was all that mattered. And the reality of it lay with Far and he was the only person that Péttur wished to be with right now. 'As a matter of fact,' Péttur thought, 'I don't think I will ever leave his side.'

"I'm on my way to Maisondepahn," Far said. "I could use some help."

"Yes. Thank you. I would be honored to ride with you, Far. Whatever you want. Whatever you need. I am at your service always," Péttur said sincerely. Far knew that he meant it. The change in his heart was true. Far wondered what had happened. He knew essentially what had happened. That part was always the same in some ways, but the way it happened was as unique as a fingerprint. He was now looking forward to the ride to Maisondepahn.

Far sent Péttur inside the house to find more provisions. He came back with some grain wafers and more dried meat that he had found. If they found no more food along the way, they would be able to sustain themselves on what they had. Péttur said little. He simply waited for Far's commands. He didn't trust himself, having seen all of the bad decisions he had made. He entrusted himself completely to Far's guidance and suddenly lived to receive a direction from him. Any desire of Far's was Péttur's command. He was so sorrowful for the pain he had caused the saçèrdōté that, Péttur himself was surprised to find, there was a strong desire to give his own life for Far if the need arose. 'Where has this come from?' he wondered to himself. But the joy that he felt in this newfound reality outmeasured anything he had ever experienced and he wanted it to last.

Péttur mounted Heiður, taking care of Far's knees, the pain of which went directly to Péttur's heart. The sorrow he felt for the pain he had caused him stayed, along with all the other sorrows that he now kept close. Somehow he knew that keeping them close was what was needed. He wished to never forget how far he had fallen and what he was capable of.

The air was cool as Far pulled Heiður out of the stable into the night. Péttur suddenly felt a chill. He had forgotten how thin his new clothes were. He decided that he didn't care, but Far noticed that something was amiss.

"Go inside and find some of Stephen's clothes," he said. "I don't know why I didn't think of it before."

A sadness struck Péttur that he himself didn't understand.

"Péttur, we have a long way to go. What is wrong?"

"I don't know," Péttur said softly, but tears were coming to the surface of his eyes.

"What is it?"

He searched his heart for the answer. This new heart had many sensitivities and expanses of feeling and thought. "It's... I think it's... I came here searching for that man. I was going to... I don't know what I was going to do. If Mag had told me to kill him, I would have killed him, Far. I don't deserve to wear his clothes. I can't."

Far turned to face Péttur. He understood what was happening. Péttur was afraid of being rejected by the Royame for what he had done. Far had seen this before and oftentimes he was right. To be forgiven by a priest was good, but what about the rest of the Royameheirs? "Péttur," he said, "Stephen is your brother now. Whatever happened in the past, you must learn to believe that. You are Royameheir. You belong to our people. Whatever we have, we share... everything. Joy, pain, belief, friendship, and clothes. Believe me. Stephen would be the first to give you whatever he has."

"Even though I would have killed him and his family?"

"Even as you committed the act, if it had happened, Péttur, but now with joy, he would give it to you, I promise. He will be so glad to meet you one day. You have no idea. What a feast we will throw that you have returned to us, Péttur. For you, it is like you have found your family, but for us, it is like a long lost brother has returned home. You understand?"

Péttur shook his head and dismounted Heiður. As Far watched Péttur disappear into the house, he wondered at how much love he could withstand. The beauty of seeing the life return to this son, dead to himself only hours ago, was beyond measure.

Péttur stepped out of the house and for a moment, Far's heart called out the name of Péttur's father. Péttur had chosen Stephen's white tunic and a long, brown coat that Steven had left behind. The clothes a little long, Péttur looked a bit childlike and completely innocent with the way his white curls sparkled in the moonlight, but he couldn't help but see his father in him. 'A new saint,' Far thought to himself.

"They're a bit big," Péttur said as he made his way back to Heiður, glancing up at Far from beneath his curls for reassurance.

"But warm, yes?" Far asked.

"Yes," Péttur smiled.

It was the smile of a child, Far decided. This new Péttur had found his lost innocence in a short time. How beautiful it was.

Péttur mounted Heiður again. "Ready?" Far asked Péttur.

"Ready," Péttur answered.

Far sensed in his voice that he was ready, not only for the trip, but to accept the protection of the Royame, as he had accepted the protection of Stephen's clothes. Far decided that this was a much better trip than the one he thought he was going to have only an hour ago. He was thankful for many things. He looked up into the sky as they began moving forward and gave thanks for the moon this night as they left the small clearing that surrounded Hyamæa and entered the forest that grew dark with each step forward. Yes, Far decided, he was glad that he was not making this trip alone with his broken knees. Maisondepahn was at least an eight hour journey if he went by the North side of the /mountain and around. King Maxamea's men were still searching the area, he knew, and Mag was still on the loose. Just as he was thinking this, Péttur said, "What do you think happened to Mag, Far?"

"I don't know. He rode fast toward the desert. He no longer has a horse. The two of you traveled all day yesterday. If I were Mag, I think I would be asleep right now, perhaps dead, but to err on the side of caution, I would say, sleeping or moving slowly in this direction. There is nothing here to sustain a man but Hyamæa."

†††

As Mag awoke from a very deep, but, he decided, unfortunately short, slumber, for a moment he forgot to wonder that he was alone. Then he realized that he was both alive and out of danger. And hungry.

He stood up and sensed that he was about to have one of those moments where one is grateful to be alive, but decided to just get to business. He looked to the West – desert. He looked to the East– forest. Ill-equipped for the desert, though that seemed to be the way the family had gone, he turned back toward the forest, having decided to cut his losses for now and return to the King with news that he had found the family. He hoped that this would be seen as a success – at least enough of one to keep him alive. He decided to return to the boat, stop at Hyamæa along the way for rest, and then head back to Halvmånen, the capitol.

Just as he was making his way to the break of trees that began the Western edge of the forest, the crow showed up again.

"You again," he said. "Well, I wasn't expecting to see you so soon." He was actually glad to see the bird, but could not express this sentiment, even in front of a creature, he reflected momentarily, but did away with the thought.

"Where's the boy?" he asked, but the bird slunk back, seeming to understand that he was not being welcomed. He seemed almost hurt by it, Mag noticed. For a moment, he felt bad. The bird did risk his life for him, for some reason. "No boy, huh? What good are you?" The bird backed away from him and was about to take flight when he heard that tone in Mag's voice – the one that meant that he wanted the crow to do something.

"Well, if you're going to stay, then be of use. I'm hungry," he said. "Go get me something to eat!" he yelled. "Go!"

The crow alighted to the top of the trees and soared into the forest. Moments later, he returned, but not with food, which Mag understood was an impossible request for a bird. "I mean, what will he bring you, Mag? Worms?" he laughed to himself. The bird held in his beak a piece of cloth dyed a deep purple, a color usually only seen on royalty, as it was a very expensive color to procure for cloth. The bird dropped the cloth into Mag's hand as he reached up for it.

"What is this?" Mag asked, turning it over to see if there was any marking on it. None. He saw that the bird seemed to be trying to tell him something, moving forward quickly and then coming back.

"Do you want me to follow you?" he asked. "Alright, friend. We'll see what you have." The crow moved fast. Mag had barely re-gained the strength to move, but he kept up with him anyway, slowly moving into a slow run. Just as he was deciding that he couldn't move any further, the crow stopped and landed on the trunk of a great tree that was surrounded by leaves.

"Well, great," said Mag. " A tree." Then he noticed that there was something strange about the way the leaves were arranged. He pushed the leaves away and found several small trunks as well as a large cloth bag full of clothes. This must have been where the crow got the piece of cloth, he said aloud to himself. "Old crow!" He yelled up at the bird happily. "Good bird," he said as he poured the bag of clothes onto the ground. The crow began to flap his wings fast with approval, flew up into the air and then came down and sat proudly upon one of the trunks. Mag took the locks for the trunks in his hands, finding nothing of interest in the bag of clothes.

He searched the ground for a rock that he could smash the locks with. Finding one, he returned to the trunks. He took the rock in his right hand and came down hard on the lock that was keeping him from the contents of the largest trunk. He struck it once. The lock did not give. He struck it a second time. Still no luck. The third time, though, he came down at just the right place and the lock broke. Hurriedly, he removed the lock from the trunk and opened the lid. His heart sank immediately as he saw nothing but books in the box. He wondered who would find these titles interesting. *History of the Royame, The Life of St. Stephen, The Lives of the Saints.* And on and on it went. Book after book. No personal writing. Sensing his master's discontent, the crow flew back a few feet.

He decided to try to open the next trunk. After a few blows, the lock gave. He lifted the lid. His stomach saw the contents before he did. Food. Lots of food. For a moment, the relevance of the mission gave way to simple, human need. Cured meats and breads. He ate his fill quickly and stored as much as he could carry on his person for the rest of the journey.

The crow flew up to him and sat at his feet, seeming to desire his approval. "Well, you couldn't expect them to leave anything of too much value behind, could you? But the meat is good," he said to the bird as he tore off a large piece of cured meat with his teeth. "You have proven yourself to be useful, haven't you?" he said. "Are you my new shadow?" he asked. That's what I'll call you then, but in the ancient language. "How is that?" he asked. "Skygge." " I will call you Skygge," he confirmed. "How do you like that?" he asked. Skygge cocked his head to the right, seeming to understand that Mag was trying to communicate. Mag pointed his finger at himself. "Mag," he said. He repeated his own name a few times. He pointed to the crow and said, "Skygge." The last time he pointed, Skygge hopped onto his finger, sensing that it was okay. Mag smiled. This was the first time he had been touched lovingly by another creature in years.

## Chapter 6

### Winds of Fortune

As they made their way toward Maisondepahn, Péttur had many questions for Far. His mind was filled with desire to know everything about the Royame. "Have you seen L'Agneau?" Péttur asked Far. "You gave your life for him. Have you seen him?"

"I've seen him in dreams," Far answered. "If he has cause to speak to you personally, it's about business, you know? Like when the general talks to a soldier, but he is always here, guiding us."

"How?" Péttur asked.

"It was a gift given to him by God," Far answered, "because of his sacrifice."

"Like what you did for me."

"Excuse me?" Far asked.

"Like what you did for me. You sacrificed yourself for me. And now I'm here with you and you're guiding me."

"Oh, I see," Far said. "Kind of like that, I guess, but his sacrifice saved the world," Far said.

"Yours saved me," Péttur said softly.

Far felt a tear form quickly in the corner of his eye. To be compared to L'Agneau was too much. He longed to love as well as him, as perfectly as him. He longed for it, though he knew that longing would have to be enough, but at times like this, he thought that perhaps at this moment, L'Agneau may be proud. "We say that if there was only one human being left on the earth, he would have done the same thing. Well, he did it for you, Péttur. I hope you know that."

"I know, Far. I know because you did it, and I want to do it for others. I want to show them what you showed me."

Now the tears were falling from Far's eyes. He was glad that he was riding in front of Péttur so that Péttur couldn't see them. "That means a lot to me, Péttur," he managed to say. Just then, something caught Far's eye – a blue light came from the floor of the forest. "A firefly?" he wondered? He pulled Heiður cautiously up to the place where the light was flickering. He saw Péttur's armor strewn about on the forest floor.

"Well, this is quite a mess," Far laughed to himself.

"Yeah, I guess, said Péttur," remembering the moment that he felt he couldn't tear the armor off of his body fast enough.

"You think we should do something about this?" asked Far.

"Yeah, I guess," Péttur said as he dismounted his horse. He picked up his helmet and looked it over. "It's so heavy," he said to Far. "I never realized how heavy it is."

"In so many ways," Far said.

Péttur took the helmet and walked over to a place where he saw a pile of leaves fallen against a tree. He thought that he would move them over, put the armor there and cover it up again. He jumped into the leaves to loosen them up, but instead of a soft pile of leaves, his legs hit something soft, but solid and he flew backwards, landing on his back. The helmet flew out of his hand as a large, black bear arose from the leaves. "What!" cried Péttur, scrambling to get to his feet.

"What is it?" yelled Far.

"Did you know that bears hide under leaves?" yelled Péttur.

"Yeah, that's how they sleep," yelled Far.

"Well, you could have told me that!" yelled Péttur.

"Didn't think of it!" yelled Far.

"Péttur, listen to me!" Far yelled, as the bear, growling, approached Péttur cautiously, swiping at him with his large claws.

"What I wouldn't give to be covered in Eiwengaard armor right now!" Péttur yelled.

"Péttur, stand up fast and throw your hands in the air!" Far yelled.

"Yeah, right!" Péttur yelled.

"Look, if my knees weren't broken…"

"Man, I am so sorry about that!"

"Just do it!" Far yelled. "Do it now!"

"How do you know this works?" asked Péttur.

"I read about it," Far answered.

"So you've never seen it work!" cried Péttur.

"If you have a better idea, let me know! If you don't then I suggest…"

Péttur leapt up from the forest floor, using all the adrenaline in his body to throw his throw his hands up in the air and yelled at the top of his lungs, "Arrrrrgggghhh!"

The bear, stunned, took a few steps back.

"Now, don't run, Péttur," Far yelled, but it was too late. Péttur ran, jumped up on Far's horse, and Far hit the reigns against Heiður's sides, clicking fast into his ear. The bear chased them on all fours for several miles before he was finally satisfied that the horse and its riders were not within his reach.

"Don't run?" Péttur asked as they had slowed down to a trot.

"Yeah, don't run. Everyone knows that," Far said.

"Not everyone," said Péttur.

"Sorry. I thought you knew. You never run from an animal like that. You back up slowly, making it seem that you are taller than the animal."

"I wasn't taller than that bear," said Péttur.

"Well, the bear doesn't know that," answered Far.

"You read it in a book?" asked Péttur.

"Yeah," said Far.
"I read it in a book."

†††

When I awoke in my mother's arms, which had relaxed a bit, I noticed, I reached up out of her head scarf and looked out upon a vast expanse of desert that drifted, seemingly, into eternity. The animals had slowed down to a gentle walk and the sun had risen upon the white, sandy dunes.

I giggled with approval at the sight of the desert. I don't know why, but my heart simply loved it and still does to this very day. My mother, hearing my laughter, looked down at me with her sea-blue eyes that sparkled like sea-blue gems in the desert sun. We stared at each other for a time. I looked out into the desert and then back at her and smiled. I reached up for her and she took me into her arms where I could see even more of the desert. I crawled up and looked beyond her back to where we had travelled.

There was no sign now of vegetation. The forest that I was so used to was starkly contrasted with this sandy expanse of plains, plateaus, and dunes. My father travelled just behind us now, since Gercek was leading. He waved at me and smiled. I reached for him, but soon realized that I would be separated from him until we dismounted from the animals, as usual.

I looked ahead and decided toward Gercek and his camel, a sight that it seemed I could look upon for ages and never grow bored of. A camel. I laughed at its long, gangly legs and the way Gercek rocked to and fro on his back. I called out for Gercek in my baby tongue, and he actually turned around. I smiled at him. We laughed together for some time.  I reached for him too, always wanting to transcend space to reach people.  Sometimes, as a babe, I could not understand why this could not happen.  It frustrated me, but I accepted it as he turned around and I focused my attention on the desert.  I looked up into the air and saw Pålitlig circling above.

My mother pointed to a point on the horizon where the speckled, sparkling dunes met the sky, and I turned my attention to the place that she was pointing toward.  I saw a figure in the waves that moved along the ground, emerged from a distorted view, and moved toward us.  Then I saw behind it many more figures.  I felt my mother's arms grow tense around me and pull me into her chest again.  I knew what this meant.  It didn't always mean danger, but perhaps.  I grew still and quiet.  I drifted down into her head scarf where I felt safer, but peaked my eyes through so that I could see.  I always needed to see everything.  Gercek stopped his camel and waited for my father to pull up beside him.

My mother pulled up to the other side of Gercek.

The first thing my father said was, "In God's hands."

"Yes," Gercek replied.  "In God's hands."

"Do you know them?" my father asked.

"Yes. They are of my tribe." Gercek answered. "They are Demudi Udi Aramad of the house of Atta."

"Good news or bad news?" my father asked matter-of-factly.

"Could be either, friend, but whatever it is, I stand with you."

"They all hate Royameheirs, right?" My father asked.

"Some more, some less, but all, yes," Gercek answered.

"Just making sure," my father said.

"Is that a bead of sweat forming at your brow?" Gercek asked, smiling.

"We're in the desert, Gercek," my father smiled back.

"Yes. But I think it was not there before," Gercek smiled again.

"Courage is fear overcome, my friend. No fear. No courage," my father said, returning to his more serious tone.

"Yes," Gercek agreed, "Only fools are without fear." His voice had also become matter-of-fact as they both stared out into the desert.

My father walked his horse over to where my mother and I sat, now that Gercek could offer no more insight into the situation. My father knew what it meant to encounter Demudi Udi Aramad in their territory. It could go either way, but we knew that we were in God's grace. The fear was always falling out of that grace and protection somehow.

My father wrapped his arm around my mother now that we were close to each other. I found myself in my favorite place – between the both of them. They looked, not at the danger in front of us, but at each other as the tribesmen approached.

"You're going to be in so much trouble," my father called out to Gercek, smiling. "Hanging out with Royameheirs."

Gercek laughed. "Yes, friend. I will die for you, but don't tell them I'm your friend, okay? Let me do the talking. I know my people. They're not ready yet, okay? I have an image to keep up. Okay?"

My father didn't answer.

"Okay?" Gercek called back.

"Okay," my father called back.

"I'll take care of this. Oh no!" Gercek cried, looking up into the sky.

We all looked up to see where his finger was pointed.

"Your bird!" cried Gercek.

We saw that Pålitlig was moving up higher into the air and moving in the direction of the tribe.

"Oh no!" Cried Gercek again. "Stupid bird."

"What's wrong?" asked my father.

"That bird is an Imamah thief, Stephen!" He said indignantly, spitting as he spoke.

"It's a what?" asked my father, clearly amused at Gercek's reaction.

"It's an Imamah thief. You know. The... the... turban. He's going to steal their turbans! And they will not be as kind as me, I assure you, Stephen. Also, he is not the welcome we should send. This is a bad idea. A very bad idea. Oh!" Gercek cried. He almost threw his whip to the ground, but thought better of it. He was clearly agitated as he watched the bird, thoroughly out of control, move across the sky, toward the mass of men. He looked at my father, as though he could do something.

"Don't look at me," my father smiled. "Pålitlig is his own bird."

"What? Pålitlig. He has a name? What does that mean?"

"Eagle," my father said.

"How creative," Gercek said.

"Well, he's an ea – "

"Yes. Yes. Well, he is also an Imamah thief. Can't you call him back or something? He stays with you, right? He is your eagle."

"He is a gift from L'Agneau and he is L'Agneau's and he is as free as you and me."

"Great."  Gercek said resignedly, regaining his composure. "Great."

As the men approached, we could see that they were 12 in number and they were all armed with swords, their faces covered by their black Imamah's, revealing only their eyes, which, as they grew closer, I could see were piercing and alert.

"Well, so far they all still have their Imamahs," Gercek said, relieved, as the group of sand dwellers drew near.  They lifted their swords into the air as they approached, balancing gracefully on the backs of their camels, reins in the other hand.  They made a formidable sight.

"There's that sweat again, Stephen," Gercek said through the side of his mouth as he raised a small light blue flag in his hand, showing that he desired peace. "Can't you control yourself?"

My father's eyes twinkled a smile that would have been imperceptible to the men headed toward us while keeping his face firmly set forward.  My mother's arm tightened around my waist.  I wriggled a bit to get more comfortable and dove down into her veil and peaked my eyes back up over the edge so that I could see. The men formed a circle around us.

"I know these men," Gercek said as they approached at a gallop.

"Is that a good thing or a bad thing?" my father asked.

"Could be either. We are family until a code is broken. We have a saying. All men are good until they are bad. In our culture, it is a great disgrace to show more leniency toward family or friends, so it matters not. Only the law matters. There is no mercy amongst the Demudi Udi Aramad." "No mercy," he repeated, seeming to go far away for a moment.

"Gercek," Their leader said. "We wondered what had happened to you. Your wife is very worried. She sent us for you."

"You didn't tell your wife?" my father asked him.

Gercek shrugged and looked at my father sheepishly, as though he now understood the error. "The spirit said go, I go," Gercek answered under his breath.

I could tell that my father did not think that this was a good answer.

"Yes," he addressed the tribesmen again," that was a foolish mistake," said Gercek. "I apologize for my carelessness. I am truly an ignorant man. But you know how women worry," he said, trying to appeal to their shared experience of women.

"Yes," said Haddar, "however, a scared lioness is more powerful and less reasonable than a sleeping one."

"Yes," agreed Gercek. "That is true, but if I may add, if the lioness is scared for no reason, she will make foolish mistakes, no?"

"Yes," agreed Haddar. "Is there no reason, Gercek?" he asked, looking in the direction of our family.

"No reason, Haddar. This family wishes safe transport across the desert. They have asked me to be their guide."

"Careful. No lying, Gercek," my father warned him quietly.

Gercek gave him a knowing look and lightly nodded in agreement.

"You made this agreement when?" asked Haddar.

"This is becoming personal, is it not?"

"Yes, Gercek," Haddar agreed, "but people travelling through our territory is usually community business, no? It is you who have made it personal – for personal reasons," he added, looking at us.

"Do they seem dangerous, Haddar? Look at them. Can their reasons be their reasons? You know our custom that a stranger may rest with us for 40 days without being asked his name."

"No one practices that, Gercek," said Haddar, but he assessed our family all the same and agreed that we did not pose a threat. He gestured for the tribesmen to lower their swords. I noticed the relieved looks on the faces of the men whose arms were growing tired. Some tried to massage their arms imperceptibly, but I noticed, being especially attuned to any suffering, which I always wished to alleviate when I noticed it.

"I apologize for any trouble, Haddar," Gercek said, honestly, "but may we please continue on to the camp in peace. I will vouch for them. They are a good family of peace."

"To the camp?" asked Haddar, shocked.

"Yes," said Gercek. They will be my guests for the night.

"No stranger may lodge with us without the permission of Asa-ari. You know that."

"Yes. I was going to ask when I retur –"

"He is gone to Maisondepahn, Gercek."

"Then I will ask Asa-aul," said Gercek.

"He is gone too," Haddar said. "They have all gone to war council."

"War council?" Gercek asked.

"Yes. War council. Many of our people were at market in Maisondepahn two days prior and were slain by King Maxamea's army, including many female babies, he said, looking at me suddenly with a stare that caused my heart to beat faster, along with my mother's. "Have you not heard?" he asked, looking still at me. My mother's grip tightened around me as my parents continued to look forward so as to not attract attention, but I felt my mother's heartbeat quicken and it seemed she wished to cry again upon hearing of more innocents slain.

"Yes, I knew that this happened, but I did not know our people –"

"Yes, our people were there," said Haddar, looking suddenly saddened.

"Then whose decision will it be?"

"Mine," said Haddar.

"Oh," Gercek said, momentarily disappointed. Then he said resignedly, "Well then, we ask for protection for the night."

"No," said Haddar, without hesitation.

"But they cannot stay in the desert in the night with this child," Haddar pleaded.

"We are in mourning, Gercek. When you arrive at camp, you will see. It would be impolite to the mourning if we invited strangers in."

"In the name of our children who died, I am sure that the camp would welcome a child, Haddar, if I may be so bold."

"No," he said looking squarely at me," you may not be so bold. You may travel forward or turn back, but you may not remain in camp with this family tonight." "It seems that little girls are bringing misfortune these days," he added, looking at me, "especially ones who need the protection of secrecy, I imagine," he said finally and kicked his camel as though he meant to leave to make his point more clearly.

It was then that one man looked up into the air and beheld a mystic sight that is not seen every day... an eagle with a snake writhing in its beak. All looked up to behold the sight. My father, whose hand was held up like everyone else's, was as shocked as everyone when as suddenly as Pålitlig appeared, the snake was just as suddenly wrapped tightly and completely around my father's arm.

The Demudi Udi Aramad drew their swords and pointed them toward my father and the snake. Words such as "Curse" and "Damned" and "misfortune" fell out of the mouths of the sand dwellers as they waited for my father to fall down dead. However, just as suddenly as the snake appeared, its head was crushed with my father's other hand... "with no sweat," Gercek would later relate, broad-smilingly, of this moment. My father calmly unwrapped the snake from around his arm, which was left wholly unharmed. My mother scarcely had time to react, but she watched, I noticed, as a queen watching a tournament whose outcome was already determined.

My father dropped the snake to the ground and Heli, without any prompting, stepped on it, crushing its writhing body so that it was finally still and silent, just like the Demudi Udi Aramad. They were all silent, staring at my father, who looked like he had just swatted a fly. He looked up to see how the negotiation was going and seemed genuinely surprised to see that everyone was now looking at him instead of at Gercek. "Oh," he said, "you think that's something?" he laughed lightly, recalling the miracles he had seen, including, among other things, men raised from the dead. "Amusing, I suppose," he said to Gercek quietly.

"Yes, Stephen, amusing," agreed Gercek, whose eyes searched the crowd slowly, waiting to see what would happen next. Then they all heard the words "snake destroyer" break the silence. "Yes, snake destroyer," agreed another voice. They lowered their swords and some began to bow their heads in reverence. Eyes looked from Haddar to Stephen, or simply lowered to the ground. A second head covering, used in their worship rituals began to cover the heads of the men. Haddar looked at the men, who all seemed to be in agreement of the sanctity of the man who sat, he decided, regally, upon the black steed.

Haddar walked his camel over to another man, perhaps the second in command, spoke privately with heads nodding, and then walked cautiously toward my father.

"Three great seers of the Demudi Udi Aramad have seen a man who is called snake destroyer in their visions," Haddar revealed to my father in explanation of what was now happening with the sand dwellers. "Most of us know of this vision," he continued. "However, not everyone knows all the details of the vision. I am one who knows *all* of the details. I invite you into our camp in obedience to our God because it is meant to be, but know, traveller, stranger, that we Demudi Udi Aramad do not fear death and that is why I invite you in — because inviting you, I know that I invite death, though most here will think that we invite a God. I will let them believe it. They are a simple and believing people and need not fear needlessly and their fear may impede the will of our God, and so I invite you, but you rest on the edge of a sword. Do you understand?"

My father nodded his understanding... and his respect for Haddar, that I could tell was there. I loved to see it so in my father's eyes. It made me feel safe.

Haddar turned to go, and then turned his camel quickly around, facing my father again, "And you will answer questions, stranger," he added and then hit his camel quickly on each side and darted forward into the desert. The tribesmen followed him, unhesitatingly, yelling, "Snake Destroyer!" in whoops and calls as they waved their swords excitedly in the air, flashing a wide, white smile at my father before they left.    Gercek looked at my father, wide-eyed and yelled, "Hail L'Agneua! Your God is truly the one true God, Stephen," he smiled. "Smart bird," he added as he struck the sides of his camel, looking up at Pålitlig, who was soaring through the air, riding the waves of the currents above. He seemed happy, I thought, though I don't know what made him seem so... perhaps the way that his beautiful wings remained spread and long and moved diagonally across the air in long, smooth strokes. He would drift far and then turn back, seemingly riding the same current in the opposite direction. Once the tribe had left, he came down closer and remained just behind my family as we headed toward the camp... to safety.

## Chapter 7

## Still Winds

The blue-lit desert sands sparkled like tiny diamonds, even in the Demudi Udi Aramad camp, where I found myself upon awaking in my mother's arms. The moon hovered above, a comforting reminder of home, I found. The tents of the Demudi Udi Aramad of Atta were all made of white-washed muslin, matching the colors of the sands around us, hiding the tribe somewhat in the crescent-shaped desert basin that they called home. Each tent was different, but they were mostly square in nature, looking clean and tidy. The desert seemed clean and the desert dwellers were very clean people, owning few things, relying mainly on their relationships with each other for sustenance.

 I awoke as we were entering the camp, so I saw what my parents and everyone saw when we entered – hundreds of sand dwellers lining our path. Though it was late and they were usually sleeping at this time, men, women, and children lined our path into the camp. Some bowed as we passed. Others simply stood with a look of questioning on their faces while some fanned us with palm leaves, as was a customary greeting for an honored guest. Some looked skeptical, the children looked sleepy, but all were looking at us. This is my first experience of civilization. Certainly this was how I felt about my parents, so I really thought nothing of it at the time. In the Royame, we were used to greeting each other with reverence. However, I remember a few eyes that were not reverent. They were quite the opposite. They reminded me of Mag's eyes, and sent me back into my mother's veil for safety.

 Haddar took us directly to the tent of council, where a young Demudi Udi Aramad boy took our animals to bed for the night.

 "You may go inside and have a seat," said Haddar to my father. "It will be up to the council to decide your fate. It is too much for me to bring on this camp by myself."

"I understand," said my father to Haddar.

Gercek stood beside my father a moment. "I am sorry, Stephen," Gercek said to my father. "I am not a member of the council. Too many headaches, you know?" Gercek said apologetically, wishing now that he had accepted the offer of council member when it came. "Now, because of my laziness..." Gercek said, ready to accuse himself of a mistake.

"Relax, Gercek. It is not in your hands," my father said calmy, then smiled at his friend.

"Yes. Yes. Sometimes I forget, friend. You will be fine. Of course you will. I must go to the bed of the angry lioness."

"Yes, you better go," said my father, smiling.

Gercek paused, not wanting to go.

"Go," my father smiled. "We will see you in the morning.

"Are you sure you don't want me to stay?" Perhaps..."

"Go," my father commanded.

"Okay. Okay," Gercek relented. "I'm going."

We watched our friend as he walked hesitantly back toward the place where we had entered the camp and then disappeared around a corner.

My father squeezed my mother and me into him as we stood in the moonlight, still for the first time in hours and surrounded by people for the first time in years. We stood like that for some time, taking in the changes, before he let go, took my mother's hand and led us toward the council tent.

We stepped inside the tent where another young boy was tending to a fire that had just recently been started, it seemed. He looked up at us shyly. My mother smiled at him and I smiled too. He smiled back and then quickly turned his gaze back to the fire. His clothing matched the tent and the sand outside. It was cold, so he had his sand-colored hood drawn up over his head, though it seemed almost too big, leaving much space around the outline of his head so that it framed his head, almost like my mother's veil. His Imamah hung around his shoulders like a long scarf.

I learned later that the Demudi Udi Aramad were never without an Imamah, never knowing when a sand storm might occur. Even at night, young sand dwellers were taught to drape it over their shoulders.

As he crouched over the fire, I was glad to see someone who was not yet an adult, but not a baby like me either. I stared at him until he seemed satisfied with the fire. He stood up and looked at it, then looked around, perhaps to see if there was anything else he could tend to. He looked at my mother, then looked away. He looked at her again. This time, my mother motioned for him to come over.

"What is your name?" she asked as she held out her hand for him to take in greeting, as is the custom of their people.

He took her hand in his and kissed it gently, then answered, "My name is Neru, my lady."

"How old are you?" She asked.

"I have 11 years, my lady," he answered, looking happily into her eyes. He looked at me for a moment.

"My name is Gayle and this is Grace," my mother said, letting me down to the sandy floor of the tent.

"Oh, she is very pretty!" said Neru, smiling. "My sister has this many years," he said. "She does not yet walk, but she crawls. Does she crawl?" he asked.

"No," my mother answered. "She does not yet crawl."

"Oh, my sister is a little older then. She is very pretty," said Neru, smiling at me all the while. I liked him very much.

"Thank you," answered my mother.

My mother could tell that Neru wanted to say something. He kept looking at my father.

"Do you have a question, Neru?" my mother asked.

"It is rude," said Neru. "I am not to speak of it. I am under orders," said Neru.

"Perhaps I can guess. If I guess, then you won't get in trouble, will you?"

He thought about it for a moment and then decided, "No. I suppose that would be alright."

"Do you want to know if he is the snake destroyer?"

"Yes, my lady, is it true? Is it really him?"

"Well, I can tell you, Neru, that when we were in the desert, a snake..."

"Dropped from the sky, from the Gods!" cried Neru.

"From an eagle's mouth," corrected my father suddenly. Neru blushed at the sound of my father's voice, which had been silent to this point.

"But still, sir, it came from the sky, yes?"

"Yes," my father agreed hesitantly. "From an eagle's mouth, it fell through the sky."

"And it fastened itself automatically to the warrior's arm."

"I am not a warrior," said my father.

"I am sorry, sir, but the snake destroyer is a warrior. He is a warrior who will come to defeat the enemies of our people. He will save us."

"I am a carpenter, Neru," said my father.

"Well, perhaps now that you have defeated the snake, you are a warrior, no? You are so strong, sir. You have fought no battle?"

"Only for a short time."

"Then you are a warrior! It is you, sir. I know it is you. I can see it. You are very handsome too," Neru added. "You must believe. We are so glad that you are here," said Neru when his eyes suddenly went to the door. He quickly moved back to the fire when he saw that the elders of the tribe were beginning to enter. He looked back at my mother and me shortly and then turned his gaze finally into the fire, thinking gladly that he had met the great snake destroyer, the liberator of their people. I could tell by the way he gazed into, though past, the fire, and smiled to himself.

"Neru," a voice barked from the opening of the tent. "That is all. I told you to start the fire, not babysit it."

Neru quickly moved toward the door, looking at our family, then moved hesitantly out of it, running to meet his friends and tell them what had just happened. Our reputation was secure in the hands of Neru, who told everyone of snake destroyer and his woman's kindness, how they spoke to him like he was a real person. "He is just like you would think," he would be saying proudly for weeks and months to come to anyone who would listen.

Haddar motioned for my mother to take a seat next to a seat at one head of a very long table that rested close to the ground. A tapestry of thick gold and black yarn lay on the ground and many soft pillows all around it. My mother thanked Haddar and laid me down on a very soft pillow and then sat down beside me. My father took his place next to my mother, placing his arm firmly around her waist. I laid my head up against his hand and he placed his hand on my head, which brought me the greatest comfort imaginable.

The rest of the men took their seats and looked at my mother and my father. One man, a tall man, sat next to me. His robe, unlike the robe of the boy, was a bright, golden yellow. I would find out later that these were the robes of the elders of the tribe. Only they were permitted to wear them. This, I came to understand, was a very important sign in the tribe. If an argument broke out, any man in a yellow robe could solve the problem. Peace was largely kept in this tribe because of the yellow robes. The man who sat beside me stole glances downward at me and smiled throughout the meeting. But when he looked at my father, his face became serious again.

I reached up for my mother, sensing that something was going on. She pulled me up and let me rest on her lap, lying against her chest. I could see everything. I was happy.

Haddar took his seat opposite my father at the other head of the table.

"Please state your name, your father's name, and your place of birth for the council," Haddar said to my father.

" My name is Stephen Christianson, son of Chris Christianson of Maisondepahn," my father stated.

"Stephen, son of Chris of Maisondepahn, you have been brought before the council this evening so that the council may determine whether you will rest with us or journey on. We will determine in this meeting, if we are able, how long you may remain with the Demudi Udi Aramad of Atta, if you are to remain with us at all. All strangers who remain with the Demudi Udi Aramad of Atta are extended the protection of the tribe no differently than if you were of the tribe with ancestors for many generations. If we invite you to remain with us, we will die for you, but also you become subject to our laws. That is why we do not invite strangers lightly into our camp as guests." "Also," continued Haddar, "there is the business of the prophecy we must discuss and consider. Will you promise to answer our questions truthfully, Stephen, son of Chris?"

"Yes. I promise," offered my father, sincerely, looking directly into Haddar's eyes and then making eye contact with the other members of the council.

Next, each member of the council stood, stated his name, his father's name, and his place of birth, just as my father had. Of course, none of this meant much to my father. They could have been the sons of thieves, for all my father knew, but my parents assumed that they were some of the best men of the tribe.

"Please tell us how you met Gercek, of the Tribe of Atta," Haddar asked my father.

My father told the tribe the story of how Gercek happened upon Hyamæa in the forest on his way to Maisondepahn and happened to run into my uncle and then led my uncle to Hyamæa.

"Why did your family not know where you were?" asked Haddar.

"I had to flee in order to protect my family," my father offered.

"Protect them from what?" asked Haddar.

"From harm," my father offered.

"Harm from whom?" asked Haddar.

"The government," answered my father, knowing this could go either way. The sand dwellers hated other governments, but trusted completely in their own.

"And why would the government wish to harm your family? Is not your government the most just, the most honest, the most fair government in all the land?" Haddar smiled, spreading his arms generously across the room, looking at each of the council members, inviting their own mocking approval, which he received generously with broad smiles and laughter.

My father and mother sat patiently, watching the scene before them unfold. Haddar waved his arm, gesturing for them to calm down, then he leaned forward a bit, inviting my father to answer.

"You heard of the tragedy of Maisondepahn," my father answered.

The room grew very quiet, as the feelings of the their own tragedy surfaced.

"Yes," answered Haddar, the gravity returning quickly to his voice.

"It was this harm that I sought to protect my family from," answered my father.

"But did your friends not suffer losses? Why did you not warn them?" asked Haddar.

I felt my mother pulling the tears back into her body as she pulled me into her.

"I did not know what the tragedy would be that I was warned of. I was warned and I left years before the tragedy occurred. You have seers in your camp, I am told. It was by mystic sight that I was warned and I heeded the warning. That is all."

My father grew tired of the questioning and invited them to be satisfied, which they were. Haddar moved on to the next question.

"And how is it that you are travelling now?"

"My home was no longer safe," answered my father.

"How did you know? More mystic sight?" offered Haddar.

"No. A friend," my father answered.

"Who is your friend?" asked Haddar.

"His name is Far Larkin. He is a saçèrdōté," my father answered.

"He did not travel with you?" asked Haddar.

"No. He did not travel with us," answered my father.

"Where is this friend?" asked Haddar.

"I'm not sure," answered my father honestly. "Perhaps Hyamæa, our home. That was the last place we saw him," my father said, looking at my mother and me.

My heart leapt at the sound of his name and my mind wandered, with my heart, to the last time I saw him. I searched my heart to see if he was still there. If he was on this earth, I knew I could feel him with my heart.

†††

"You know, Far, when I was a little boy, I wanted to be a saçèrdōté," Péttur said, breaking a long silence that had lasted, Far noted, the length of the moon across the sky. "Since the night I saw the beautiful lady. I guess that was a dream or something, but since I saw her, I wanted to be a saçèrdōté."

"What lady?" Far asked.

"Oh, it was this... she was the most beautiful, pure woman I have ever seen. Her voice. I will never forget her voice. After I heard her voice, no other woman's voice has ever been able to move my heart.

"You saw her."

"Who?"

"L'Agneau's mother."

"He has a mother?"

"Everyone has a mother, Péttur," Far laughed.

"Right. That was his mom?"

"Yes. It sounds like her. She came to you? That's very special, Péttur. What did she say? It's important that you remember as well as you can."

"Oh, yeah. I could never forget. The whole thing is so clear. It's like it happened yesterday. I was asleep and then I woke up. I know that I was awake. I woke up and I saw her standing beside my bed. I sat up and she smiled at me. I had such a feeling of peace. She touched her hand to my heart and I heard this voice say, "This heart is for me.""

Far stopped the horse and turned around to face Péttur. "Really, Péttur?"

"Yes," Péttur said. "And you know, with all the terrible things that I've done, I've never given my heart to another woman. I realized that tonight as I was laying on the forest floor. No woman has ever swayed me. I think they're beautiful and everything, but if you had seen her. If she had done that to you, you wouldn't have let another woman have your heart either, but I never really thought about it. It's just always been for her. After I killed my father..." Péttur choked on the words as they came out, and then he wept as he said, "I couldn't feel her anymore. I had always felt her in my heart somehow, even if I wasn't noticing it, but after I did that..." He paused. "Far," Péttur said.

"Yes, Péttur."

"I killed my father, Far. I killed my own Father."

He stopped the horse again. "You are forgiven, Péttur," Far said.

"Would you offer me the sacrament of reconciliation, Far?"

"Of course, Péttur. Is there anything else besides this that you would like to be forgiven for? Péttur suddenly had a rush of memories of things that he knew were wrong that he had done. He told them all to Far and Far lifted his hand over Péttur's head and said the words over him that brought down the special grace that cleansed his soul.

Péttur immediately felt better. The sorrow was still there, but his mind was clear— it was not heavy anymore— just pain mixed with joy somewhere deep within him.

After they had gone down the road a ways, Far said, "That's very special, Péttur. That experience you had."

"It's too bad, I guess." Péttur said.

"What Is?" Far asked.

"I think maybe she meant for me to be a saçèrdōté. I don't suppose that will ever happen now," Péttur said. "What a waste."

"You'd be surprised at who L'Agneau chooses for his friends," Far laughed.

Péttur wondered at how he could be laughing seemingly in the face of murder.

"What do you mean?" Péttur asked.

"Well, let's just say you wouldn't be the first saçèrdōté that he called who had committed that crime. As a matter of fact, one of his first followers killed many Royameheirs. L'Agneau knew he didn't know what he was doing though. You know? I mean, you can't blame kids too much. We're all kind of in the dark here. He knows that. He's very forgiving of people who are sorry for what they've done. You'd be surprised."

"So you think there's still a chance?"

"Well, if his mother's pulling for you, I'd say there's a good chance. And if you've been faithful to that love, as you say you have, I'd say there's a great chance."

Péttur's face glowed. He felt the love for the lady grow in his heart. If her son was anything like Far, he thought that he would do anything for him too. He thought about where he was just hours ago... on the forest floor, alone with no family and nothing but bad memories and pain. How had things changed so suddenly? Was this what his father had been trying to explain to him all those years? Why couldn't he see it? "I always have to learn everything the hard way," he said to himself. "If only I had done what he had said. If only..." he stopped himself. "But if anything had changed, would I be here right now? Would I know the beauty of this moment?" He decided he wouldn't change anything. He would just accept everything as it was. The amount of pain and suffering he had experienced seemed to be the amount of joy that had been given to him in return, somehow, though they both lived together. If truth was the answer to staying here, then, he decided, he would do anything to stay here.

"Who are those people?" Péttur asked.

"What people?" Far asked.

"The people who lived in that house."

"Oh. They are a very holy family," Far answered. "Friends of the lady and L'Agneau."

"Royameheirs."

"Yes, Royameheirs."

"They have a little girl, right?"

"Right," Far answered.

"And she's supposed to be special or something, right?"

"Right," Far answered again.

"Well, is she?"

Far stopped the horse again. He turned and looked at Péttur. It was the first time Péttur had asked for Far's trust, really. Very few people alive truly knew the truth about Reina, but Far believed in this new Péttur. He believed that it was true. After a moment, he looked into Péttur's eyes, and said, "Yes."

Somehow, Péttur knew that when Far told him this, by telling him this, it meant something. It meant that Far trusted him. He felt the responsibility of it. He knew that Far had risked his life for the family and now it meant, Péttur knew, that he would too. He had risked his life for evil. How much more now would he risk his life for good? If this family was worth Far's life, whose life Péttur had decided, was worth far more than his, then this family was certainly worth his life.

"Why is she so special?" Péttur asked. "So many have died because of her. I couldn't imagine growing up knowing that all those children's lives had been given for mine. How will she live with that? I hope that she is as special as they say."

"Well, all babies are special, Péttur," Far answered.

"Right, but not all babies are being hunted by King Maxamea's army."

"True."

"It is dangerous to quote prophecy, Péttur, but there is prophecy that..."

"That a queen will reign over the earth and she will reconcile many people. I know. You think the Kiläl don't know? We know. I mean, they know. So that's it though? She helps people get along and King Maxamea wants her dead?"

"I guess he's afraid of something. There's a rumor that his own prophets have foreseen that she will be his downfall. This has nothing to do with the Royame. I don't know. I just do what I'm told. I don't think about it too much."

"You have orders on this?"

"I have orders on this."

"Is she a queen?"

"That's the thing about prophecy. Everyone finds out how clueless they were and how many wrong thoughts they had after everything comes to light, so it's best to just take things as they come. There are kings and queens in the lineage of the Royameheirs, but who they are is hidden now. All of our records were destroyed a long time ago. Perhaps the Royame beyond this world knows, or perhaps she is anointed from above. I will share this with you. You are one of five people in the world who know this and I expect it to remain that way. Do you understand?" Far asked.

Péttur nodded his head in agreement.

"One night I awoke from a dream and knowledge of her was put into my heart. I know you understand this, so.... It's hard to explain, but it was like I understood her spirit. She is my God child and I baptized her, but knowledge of her reality was given to me, entrusted to me. She is of royal lineage. Somehow. I don't know how, but she is. And she is special. This is my path though. You should not worry about it," Far told Péttur. "You have your own path to worry about right now."

"Your path is my path, Far." Péttur said.

"I'm honored," Far said, "but you will have many things to do without me if you are to be a saçèrdōté."

"You really think it could happen?" asked Péttur.

"The greatest miracle has already happened, Péttur," Far said.

"Couldn't I stay with you though?" Péttur said. "Maybe I won't be a saçèrdōté then. Maybe I can just stay with you."

"Ask the lady. She knows," Far laughed.

"What do you mean, ask her?"

"Ask her."

"You think she'll answer?"

"If what you say is true, I'm sure of it."

"Okay. I will then," Péttur answered matter-of-factly.

"Where are they?" Péttur asked.

"Who?"

"The family. Reina. Where did they go?"

That feeling of protectiveness rose up within Far again. He trusted Péttur's conversion, but it was tested with the things closest to him. But if he didn't trust it, who would? He thought to himself.

"They went to the desert, Péttur."

"The desert? How will they cross the desert?" Péttur asked.

"God knows," Far answered.

"He sent them there." Péttur acknowledged.

"Yes, he sent them."

"Then they will be fine."

"Yes. They will be fine." Far agreed.

"But Mag..."

"For some reason, I am not worried about him, so I think that is okay. And I know Reina is okay."

"How do you know?"

He smiled to himself. "I just know."

"Far?" Péttur asked, hesitantly.

"Yes, Péttur." Far said.

"Do you think that my father forgives me, Far?" Péttur was re-living his past in light of his newfound beliefs.

This was a long, wonderful part of the process, Far knew, and would last for some time.

"He is with L'Agneau. There is no room for unforgiveness where he is, Péttur. You must believe that, Péttur," he said. Suddenly, his horse stopped. He heard the same thing his horse heard. It was far off, but it was strong. It seemed almost like the ground was moving. "But who would be traveling at this time of night?" Far asked himself. He and Péttur had decided to do most of their traveling at night to avoid company and questions.

"What is it, Far?" Péttur asked.

"Do you hear that?" he asked.

"Umm, yes? I hear something, but it's kind of strange."

"Like it doesn't belong."

"Yeah, like it doesn't belong."

"Right."

Péttur hopped down from his horse and put his head to the ground.

"I would join you down there, but..."

Péttur looked up. "Have I said that I'm sorry about your legs?" he smiled, though a touch of sorrow was perceptible behind the smile.

"Not in the past hour," Far smiled sheepishly.

"I'm sorry," he said, then placed his ear back to the ground. Péttur's eyes closed, then a look of resignation came over his face.

"An army," Péttur said.

"How many?" Far asked.

I'm not sure. Maybe 10. Maybe 20.

"How far?"

"Maybe a mile, if that."

"That's close," affirmed Far.

"And they're on our path. I'm pretty sure. They must be coming from Maisondepahn, or another city close to it. What do you want to do?" asked Péttur.

Far looked around for options. They could hide, they could run back toward the house, or they could walk calmly into the lion's mouth and hope to find a way out. He proposed all three to Péttur. They both agreed that number three was the option most likely to get them home. Far looked Péttur over.

"You are a penitent," Far said to Péttur.

"A what?" asked Péttur.

"A penitent," said Far. "Someone who is sorry for your sins."

"Okay. That's true," said Péttur.

"Good," said Far. Take that dirt and rub it all over your body, starting with your face and your hair, to show how sorry you are."

"What?" asked Péttur.

"I'm ordering you as your saçèrdōté to rub dirt all over your face and body until your countenance is as black as your sins," said Far. "And so they won't recognize you," he added.

"People really do that?" asked Péttur.

"Yes, they really do that," said Far.

Péttur walked into the forest and found a small puddle where some dirt had mixed with water and covered his face and hair with it. He put it all over his arms and legs and returned to Far for approval.

"Overdid it a bit," said Far, motioning for Péttur to come to where he stood. "You look like a swamp monster," he smiled, wiping some of the mud from his face. "So what do you think the chances are that you will be recognized?" asked Far.

"Like this?" Not likely, said Péttur. "Not unless it's one of my captains," said Péttur.

"How many did you have?" asked Far.

"Three," said Péttur. "Including Mag."

"Okay," said Far. Penitents walk. Walk beside the horse. We'll place this in the hands of L'Agneau."

As Péttur mounted his horse, Far reminded, "Whatever happens, Péttur, we hand this over to the Royame. Whatever happens." He looked at Péttur for concurance.

Péttur assured Far with a broad smile that whatever happened was fine with him. "The Royame!" Péttur said emphatically.

"The Royame," Far nodded, and they walked boldly forward, into their fate.

CHAPTER 8

EAST WIND

The man who sat next to me during the council meeting was slowly becoming my best friend. He looked at me more than he looked at Haddar, twinkling a smile at me often. Twice he tried to tickle my foot. I saw Haddar throw a few glances at him, but he was undeterred, seemingly resigned to leave the outcome to those who were paying attention. There were many who honestly seemed to be trying to follow the meeting in order to come to a decision. I later found out that the ones who were truly invested in the council, such as Haddar, were people who knew the full prophecy and what it might mean to keep us with them in the Atta camp.

I looked at Haddar and decided that I liked him. He was a man of principal, I could tell. He had the same look on his face that my father would have when he was trying to make any important decision. I recognized the passion in his voice as something that meant that important things were happening and he was fully invested in trying to make the right decision. It was this kind of passion that led men to sacrifice their lives – in life and in death. I smiled up at him and for a moment our eyes caught each other's. He looked from me to my friendly neighbor, giving him a glance of understanding that was imperceptible to all but me and Haddar. Haddar's softness lived somewhere underneath the heated speech and I knew in that moment the outcome of the debate, though it would last three hours more.

"Our tribesman, Gercek, is well-respected in the tribe as a man of prudence and wisdom. It is not like him to break the laws of our tribe. Did you ask him to meet you at this unusual time last evening?" asked Haddar.

"No," my father answered honestly.

"Never?" asked Haddar again.

"Never." answered my father.

I saw that the same men who seemed invested in the meeting seemed to readily accept this, believing in the spiritual world, but the man sitting next to me suddenly became incredulous at this answer and was happy to implicate my father and Gercek in conspiracy and lying.

"Then how did this come to be?" asked the man next to me, whose attention I lost completely. He moved his elbows onto the table and leaned forward toward my father. All of the tribesmen looked at my father for an answer.

My father breathed resignedly, the way he always did when he was about to speak to people of the Royame, leaving his life in the hands of fate, prepared to give it up if necessary. "I do not know your people well, but I have heard of your great faith," my father answered. "The God we worship is, I believe, the same God." he went on. "My God, like yours, is a God of miracles. I believe that it was a miracle. For my family was in grave danger when Gercek appeared on the horizon of the desert."

At the word "danger" the entire council awoke to enter a plea. "They cannot stay." "I have heard enough." "They must leave at once." The council seemed to be united, since all of the sleepers had awoken at the first sign of danger to enter a plea to avoid it. However, I noticed that the same men who believed my father's story of the miracle also remained quiet. They seemed like a small, but powerful minorty.

My mother looked to my father. A hint of worry almost entered her eyes before he cast it away with his own – and a slight smile. He took her hand to steady her. She relaxed, but put her arm more firmly around me. Then a man spoke— a man who had not spoken to this point. He was a small man with grey hair. I had noticed him because his eyes were wise and full of knowledge, but it seemed that no one else at the council payed any attention to him, until just the smallest sound came from his throat. It was really less than a sound. It was more of a perceptive clearing of the throat, but at this small sound, all other sounds stopped. The room took on the spirit of silence and listening. All eyes turned to him. His name was Abu Atta, meaning son of Atta. He was descended from the father of the tribe and was offered the role of leadership, but having received from their God the mark of the elect, he became a spiritual leader of the tribe and was well-respected and consulted about all matters of importance in the tribe, even by the leader, his younger brother. His yellow robe was the dullest one in the room, having been worn the longest, and as he spoke, his bushy, gray eyebrows became a focus as his eyes often drifted downward in humility and concentration.

"My brothers," he said. "Please do not be so hasty in your decision-making." There was a pause that would have normally signalled others to fill the silence; yet, everyone remained motionless. "This young family's lives are in your hands and you know not what lives these are," he said plainly, looking directly at me as he said these words. He paused for a moment, looking down and then upward, past the room. "We must pray to know the answer to this question. The avoidance of danger is often the path that leads to it, so I ask you not to make your decision on this matter in this way." The words came slowly from his mouth and fell upon the hearts of all listening, transforming them as he spoke. "When you look at this family, wonder not who they are or what the cost will be if they remain with us, but what our God is asking you to do. If you are not clear on this, then I ask you to make no decision, especially one that is based on fear." He then sat back from the table and sunk back down into his thoughts, becoming unnoticeable again.

The man beside me, who seemed to be somewhat impetuous, spoke. "If you know something, old man, then tell us so that we can make a decision. We know that they say that this is the man of the prophecy, the snake destroyer, but you high council members have kept the prophecy to yourselves. It hasn't mattered until now, but now it matters, so if you know something that will help us to see what you see, then speak." I suddenly saw the part of my father who is a warrior in this man.

This seemed to be an opinion that was shared by all members of the council who did not know all the details of the prophecy. The crowd began to speak again. "Yes, let us hear!" "It is time we knew!" "Secrets like this should not be kept from the council!" "Let us hear this prophecy!" They were adamant, but no amount of pressure would sway the High Council, who sat calmly, looking upon the rest of the council members with fatherly and concerned eyes.

The high council members looked calmly to each other and then looked to the crowd. They looked from Haddar to Abu Atta, and rested momentarily on the other members of the high council, but when everyone saw Haddar looking to Abu Atta, their eyes rested again on the little man enclosed in the folds of his robe, his hands crossed gently over each other, his eyes looking down into the past, the present, and the future.

He cleared his throat again, seeming to prepare to speak, once again silencing the members of the council whose voices suddenly muted, but they all leaned forward, waiting for Abu Atta to tell them a story. For the Demud Udi Aramad love nothing more than a good story. Nights and days were spent in storytelling. The elders of the tribe were all master storytellers, handing the history of their people down from generation to generation with stories. Abu Atta was perhaps the greatest of the storytellers, his stories always rich in symbols that the children would talk about and try to understand for days after they had heard one of them. The faces of the council members all became like those of little children, their eyes wide with expectation, as Abu Atta looked deep into himself for the words.

"How this rumor of the snake destroyer came to be public myth, I do not know," Abu Atta said, seeming to count to ten before moving from one sentence to the next. The faces of the young men of the council suddenly fell, though the hope for revelation was still there. "I will tell you a story," said Abu Atta. At this, the entire council leaned forward and they could not help but show their child-like excitement that they were receiving, perhaps a new story, from Abu Atta.

"Not so long ago, but longer than most of you can remember," he began, in his slow, steady voice, "there was a young man."

"The snake destroyer?" asked one young man. Everyone was clearly perturbed by his question, but looked to Abu Atta for the answer.

"No," he said decidedly. "He was the Serpent Slayer," Abu Atta continued. "Or so it was said of him from the time that he was young; for when he was born, he was born with a red serpent right here on his forehead," he said, pointing to the middle of his own.

"A chosen one" one of the men said.

"Yes," Abu Atta agreed. "A chosen one." "All his life, everyone told him that he was the Serpent Slayer, but there was one problem," Abu Atta said. "He was blind."

The men looked at Abu Atta. "Blind?" they asked.

"Yes, he was blind. Well, the people had all been expecting the Serpent Slayer for some time. The Serpent Slayer was prophecied for many years, so you can imagine how they felt. Here was their Serpent Slayer, and he was blind."

"Oh, yes, they must have been very disappointed, Abu Atta," agreed the man beside me.

"Very," he said.

"But he was clearly the one who was prophecied. They could tell by the mark. Many doubted, of course, and looked still for the Serpent Slayer, but there were a few who still believed that it was him," Abu Atta told the expectant crowd.

There was a great serpent who lived within distance of their village and it came once a year to feed on the villagers, so it was very important, the Serpent Slayer. Their best warriors had not been able to defeat the serpent."

"That is terrible, Abu Atta," said one of the younger members.

"Yes, it is terrible," he agreed. "So the young man listened to this prophecy every year and every year the serpent came and fed on the villagers. Every year the people would come to his mother and ask, 'Is he ready to defeat the serpent?' Every year his mother would tell them, "He cannot even defeat his own serpent. How do you expect him to defeat that one?' For the young man was very bitter that he was meant to be the great Serpent Slayer, but God had made a mistake and made him blind. All he ever thought about was what a wonderful life he was supposed to have had as a great warrior, but instead he was stuck in his feeble body."

"Yes, Abu Atta, that is true," one man said.

"Yes, sometimes we feel bitter," agreed the storyteller. "But one evening while the young man was sleeping, a light came from above. It told the Serpent Slayer that he would be given his sight back, but it would not be like the sight of everyone else. It would be a secret sight, but first, he would have to give thanks to God for all that he had suffered from being blind."

"Thankful?" Asked the young boy. "What do I have to be thankful for? I have spent my entire life listening to people tell me that I was meant for something great, but I have not even been able to do the simplest thing."

"You have much to be thankful for," said the light. "You have learned what it means to be weak. Now you will be able to know what it means to be strong. Those who have always been strong may know what it is to be strong, but they will never know the meaning of their strength, so when you are strong, you will be thankful and protect the weak. But you must always remember that if you misuse the sight that you are given or if you are not thankful for your weakness, you will lose your strength."

"That is right, Abu Atta. That is how it is," agreed the man beside me.

"Yes, that is how it is," agreed Abu Atta.

"But when the boy woke up," he continued, "he was still blind."

"This is not right," the boy thought to himself. The light said that I would be able to see. When his mother entered the room that morning to check on him and see what he wanted for breakfast, he could not see her, but he felt a great sadness in his heart. When she left the room, the sadness left. When she came back into the room, the sadness returned.

"Mother," he asked her, "is something troubling you?"

"No," she replied, "but he knew that she was lying. He didn't know how he knew, but he knew.

"Mother, please tell me what is wrong," he said.

"Do not be troubled, Sardi," she said, "you have enough sorrow, son."

"I must know, Mother," he pleaded.

"If you must know, my sorrow is that you are sorrowful," she said. My son has never been happy a day in his life that I know of, except when he was a baby," his mother said, crying.

"Do not worry, Mother. I am now thankful for my blindness," he said. "Because I have known a great weakness, now I will know what strength is," he told her. "I am the serpent slayer, mother. I have defeated the serpent that was destroying us, my own bitterness."

She embraced him and cried tears of joy.

"Yes," a voice remarked. "A mother would be very happy for this change."

"Yes," agreed Abu Atta.

"After that day," Abu Atta continued, "strangely enough, the serpent never returned to that town to feed on the villagers. Neru told people the story of how he slayed the serpent within with the help of God and the people of the town made it a holy town under the protection of God."

Sighs of understanding went through the room. "Does he mean this man is not the snake destroyer?" I heard some say. "But he did destroy a snake," some said, sounding indignant. Then Abu Atta made the tiniest of sounds in his throat, and the room was silent again.

"People need so much to talk about something and then they believe in it. Then they make decisions based on it. Then they are living a life that is based on myth, a life that is not true." With each word, the council members seemed to feel convicted of some crime. Their eyes moved from Abu Atta to the floor and then looked up, periodically, hoping that after the rebuke, would come the truth.

"It was fifty years ago when this rumor of the snake destroyer came to be in this tribe. I tell you that it was never meant for the ears of man. It is only a myth in our tribe. If you will honor and protect the lives of these people, you must do it based on your own virtue, not a myth. More dangerous than man basing his life on lies is man living his life to fulfill a myth. I will not breathe more life into this rumor. Not here, not now, not ever. This is a family. They are the friends of Gercek. She is a child like our own who were slain. They travel away from the danger of a bad government. Make your decision based on these facts and your own conscience and nothing more. You cannot understand the prophecy until it has come to pass, so listen to your own hearts. That is where you will find the answer." Abu Atta had spoken and he was done. He sat back into his robes and cast his eyes back to the ground, into his thoughts.

The room remained silent. My friend looked away from the table and somewhere past Abu Atta, who sat directly across from him. The members of the high council sat back into their robes as well. The decision had been made, it seemed, concerning the prophecy. They would not hear of it in this council meeting. The council began to murmer underneath their breaths their disapproval of this decision, though no one seemed to have the courage to disagree outright with the decision of Abu Atta.

I saw a slender, sweet-faced man looking around, trying to find the courage to speak. Finally, he cleared his throat like Abu Atta, though it did not have the same effect on the council. He spoke, "It is said..." he spoke into the din. The people around him quieted and listened and then slowly quieted the rest of the tribe.

"It is said," said the man again. The crowd grew silent. "It is said that the snake destroyer will bring destruction to our tribe," said the man. "We should at least say what we are thinking. I have heard the prophecy and I will make my decision based on what I have heard because I was there tonight when the deadly snake was dropped by the eagle's mouth onto the arm of the man who sits here with us. From the sky it came. And before the snake struck, the man pulled the deadly snake from his arm and crushed its head in his fist. While the snake still was quick with life, he threw it to the ground and the man's horse stomped the life out of the snake. We all know that usually a horse is threatened by a snake, but this horse stomped it," the man said decidedly, as though he had made his decision.

"I have heard it said that the snake destroyer will be the savior of our people," said another voice, this time coming from another young man who had witnessed the death of the snake.

The murmuring began again, as the council members all began sharing stories that they had heard regarding the snake destroyer. "He is supposed to bring peace," said another voice loudly.

"How can he both destroy us and bring us peace?" asked one voice above the others. "That does not make sense!" he cried.

Abu Atta cleared his throat again. This time it took a little bit longer for the agitated crowd to grow silent, but they still deferred to the voice of their mystic leader.

"You see that each man has heard according to his own heart or according to his luck this prophecy of the snake destroyer. So it is that if you heard the details of the prophecy, you would hear according to your own heart. Make your decisions as you will based on your own experience... of what you have seen, of what you have heard, of what your heart tells you, but also do notice how ridiculous you sound and try, if you can, to not be ridiculous." His gaze turned from the horizon of the tent to my father. This was the first time Abu Atta had turned his gaze to a person during the council meeting. All eyes fell onto my father. "Stephen, son of Chris," he said, "it is prophesied in our tribe that you will be the destroyer, the savior, and the peacemaker of our people. What have *you* to say to this?" he asked my father calmly.

My father smiled slightly at Abu Atta, seeing in him, I knew, a kindred spirit. "Dear man," my father said, smiling ever-so-slightly, "I am only a carpenter, trying to keep my family safe."

"You see," said Abu Atta to his fellow tribesmen, "that is a great deal that you ask of Stephen, son of Chris. You all are glad that he does not take the prophecy to heart, aren't you? With a welcome like that, an average man would surely think himself something very special and likely destroy us all, don't you think?" he smiled. "So this is not an average man," he spoke finally, sinking back into his robes again, stealing a short glance of approval at my father, which was only, I'm sure, seen by my mother, my father, and me.

This time, before the tribe could comment on Abu Atta's appraisal of the situation, Haddar spoke.

"I believe we have learned as much as we may learn this evening," said Haddar forcefully, inviting anyone to argue with him. Because of the finality in his voice, no one did. "It is time for us to come to a decision. If you believe that we should give Stephen, son of Chris, and his family the protection of our tribe, give the sign of approval."

At this, the right hands, formed into fists, of the entire high council, 4 men, and two men of the low council, went up into the air. Six in all. My father looked around the table to see what had happened. He did not know what it meant, but in the council meetings of our people, it would be bad news. 7 sat with their hands on the table, the majority. The unity of the high council unnerved the men in the majority, but they held fast to their positions, straightening their backs and puffing their chests out to show that they were strong in their decisions, in spite of the high council's unanimity.

"All against," Haddar said.

The seven men raised their left hands, palms forward, signifying that they wished to let the issue – us – go.

Haddar, who apparently could not vote, being the leader of the council, spoke. "The council has spoken," he said, unable to hide the disappointment in his voice as he spoke.

My mother looked at my father with a look of wondering. He tried to smile again, but the lines of worry could not be hidden from his eyes.

My friend looked down at me, and then away. His was one of the hands that was for us. The man who reminded the council that the snake destroyer was meant to destroy their people voted to keep us here. Perhaps the words of Atta to forgo the prophecy and vote based on conscience went to his heart. He smiled a half-smile at me, then turned finally, along with everyone else, toward Haddar, the voice of the council.

My mother's eyes caught Haddar's, noticing the disappointment in his voice, pleading with him to do something. He shook his head "no" and looked down into his robe. Everyone, especially those who had voted against keeping us in the protection of the tribe, looked away from us. We searched the faces for any person who would look at us. My mother and father looked at each other, searching for the meaning of the council meeting, then they both looked at me. They forced a smile, but I could tell that they were worried. They accepted the situation, closed their eyes and handed everything over to the Royame.

## Chapter 9

## Grey Wind

In all the years that Péttur had been with the Kiläl, he didn't remember having seen the look on their faces that he now saw. Even in the moonlight, the mirror of the Kiläl faces told him that he looked ridiculous. Usually the Kiläl were simply brutal with strangers, but with a holy man and a..."

"What did you call him?" asked the captain gruffly, unable to mask the curiosity in his voice.

"A penitent," answered Far matter-of-factly. Péttur saw Far now in a new light, through the eyes of the Kiläl. He looked like a warrior, a general of an army, with his sash decorated with the emblems of the Royame, but wearing the cloak and hood of a holy man. One was hesitant to mess with either a warrior or a holy man, but the seeming combination of both, Péttur could tell, was keeping the Kiläl at a careful distance, though there were significantly more Kiläl – fifteen of them, Péttur counted. Even if it didn't last long, anything that could make a Kiläl captain hesitate was worth noting.

"What's that?" asked the captain, looking disdainfully at Péttur as his head scanned him from head to foot. Péttur recognized Gringar, who always travelled in full armor, though the helmets were usually saved for battle. His helmet, affixed to the back of his horse's saddle, was shaped like a mad boar's head with real boar tufts that came out of the top, so it was easy to recognize him, but it seemed that he had not yet been recognized by the Kiläl. He didn't know if he would, in fact, be able to identify a Kiläl soldier who was completely out of his uniform, as he himself was. The thought brought him some slight and brief comfort.

"A penitent is a person who is sorrowful for the sins and crimes that he has committed, so he covers himself in soot or dirt to show others that he is sorrowful for his sins," explained Far, using, Péttur noticed, a teacher's voice.

"What sins and crimes has he committed?" asked Gringar.

"The usual," replied Far. "It is not unusual to sin in this life is it?" he asked. "A man's sins are his own business, though, wouldn't you agree, sir?"

Gringar couldn't argue, though it seemed he wanted to, due to the extreme nature of Péttur's countenance. But he seemed satisfied that the saçèrdōté and the penitent posed no threat and lowered his weapon. The other soldiers kept their weapons up.

"Where are you going and where are you coming from?" asked Gringar.

"We are on our way to Maisondepahn, sir, and we are coming from a friend's home."

When Far tells the story, he says that this is where he began to sweat. The saçèrdōté's obligation to always and under all circumstances tell the truth makes for an always interesting life. Under pain of death, Far Larkin had sworn to himself to never lie under any circumstances. He always said that if you moved that line once, under any circumstance, especially as a saçèrdōté, you would be tempted to move it again, until the line to heaven was neither straight nor guaranteed.

The word 'home' sparked the interest of Gringar. "What home?" he asked.

"Maybe a day's journey along the trail," said Far, thinking to himself how glad he was that the family was gone and deciding that if his life ended here, it was worth it.

Gringar turned to one of his men and spoke a few words into his helmet. After exchanging a few sentences, he turned to Far. "We are looking for 2 soldiers who travelled this way. Have you seen them?"

Far looked at Péttur. "2 soldiers, you say. No, can't say that I have. Friends of yours?" asked Far.

"I'll ask the questions, saçèrdōté," snapped Gringar.

"They would have been traveling along this trail. We have seen that they came this way. How long have you been traveling the trail?" asked Gringar.

"This night," said Far.

Gringar turned back to the same soldier and spoke to him again in the Kiläl tongue.

"We don't believe you, saçèrdōté," Gringar huffed at him.

"By the oath of my office, I have sworn to never lie," answered Far. "I will die rather than lie," Far answered sincerely.

"Those are good words, saçèrdōté, but why would I believe that they are true? Every man will lie if their life is at stake," answered Gringar finally.

"If I lie to you, I will forfeit my life," answered Far. By the laws of my God, to lie is to lose your soul, so I would not lie to you."

"It doesn't matter, saçèrdōté. You say that there is a house this way?"

"Yes, said Far."

"I will let you go, saçèrdōté. We don't need the extra weight of you and your ... penitent," he snorted at Péttur. Far says that when he heard those words, he began to breathe again and he was glad he was on horseback because he was sure that even if his knees had been strong, they would have buckled.

"Thank you, sir," replied Far.

"Don't thank me, saçèrdōté. We've wasted enough time with you," he said as he kicked the sides of his horse and flew past Far and Péttur, into the forest.

Far and Péttur watched as the Kiläl traveled down the pathway.

"I thought you couldn't lie," Péttur managed to say to Far through his bated breath.

"I can't," said Far.

"But you said..."

"The way to life is narrow, Péttur," Far smiled sheepishly as he gently clicked in Heiður's ear and brushed his sides, moving gently into the forest. "I saw a wizard and a Royameheir when I saw the two of you. I didn't see two soldiers. If he had been more specific with his questions, we may have been in trouble."

"Alright," Péttur said resignedly.

"Alright," Far smiled. "Always deal in actual truth, Péttur," Far said, moving cautiously down the path as they moved away from the Kiläl soldiers. "The truth shall set you free," he laughed to himself.

Péttur's body suddenly tensed, as he remembered..."Far, the armor!" he yelled quietly into Far's ear.

"I know, Péttur," he whispered back to him as he looked back over his shoulder to see the last Kiläl soldier disappear behind the trees. "Hold on, Péttur," he said. "We're going to fly." And with that, he clicked hard and fast in Heiður's right ear, leaned forward, tapped his sides with his feet, noted momentarily the searing pain in his knees as he did so, and they flew down the path. The animals nearby saw nothing but a fast, grey wind.

†††

Far says that he knew that they would only have about a 15 minute head start before the Kiläl soldiers realized who they were, so he rode as fast as he could, but he was preparing himself for death as he rode because with the weight of two men on his back, Heiður could only ride at perhaps three-quarters of his normal speed and the speed of the Kiläl horses who, though weighted down with armor, were stronger than any other horse living, as they learned to run with that armor from the time they were colts and so gained strength and speed in spite of the armor. It was said that a Kiläl horse without armor could out-run any horse alive and sometimes, if run without their armor, would have heart attacks because their hearts would literally burst, the horses being unable to notice the signs of exhaustion that a normal horse might notice.

All of these facts went through Far's mind as he rode. He wondered how much speed Péttur could pick up if he let Péttur go on without him. He was prepared to make that sacrifice if it would make a difference. He knew that Péttur wouldn't allow it. He was too attached to him and too loyal. He turned around to ask, but knew the answer and decided not to cause Péttur the distress. He clicked again in Heiður's ear and gently stroked his side with his boot, urging him to go faster. He and Péttur both leaned forward. The trees were a blur as they moved quickly past them. The ache in his legs as he tried to hold onto Heiður's sides as they rounded corners without slowing down was growing almost unbearable. Once in a while he cried out, but he would try to mask it as a labored breath. Péttur says that he knew exactly what was happening and every cry of Far's was like an arrow piercing his heart. His new heart was so sensitive to the pain he had caused Far and looked for any opportunity to relieve it, but there was nothing he could do but hold on.

They both watched the trail as Heiður rocked down the path, holding their bodies down as far as they could bend to avoid the branches of the trees that hovered over the path. They still received, however, tiny scratches on their hands and faces. As the sweat slipped into the tiny cracks, the sting was welcomed by Stephen as a sign that they were still alive and for a tiny moment in time, the greater danger yielded to the nerves in his body that asked him to acknowledge the tiny wound of the present, which he did gladly.

†††

It was not Gringar, but his second in command, who noticed the litter of metal on the floor of the forest. Gringar, at the time, was looking down into the moonlight and shadows passing through his horse's armor, wondering if he had made the right decision – letting the holy man go. It was very strange to see anyone on a trail as hidden as this and he was sure that there was something strange about the travellers – something beyond the fact that one of them was covered in mud. And something was bothering him about the penitent, something he couldn't quite put his finger on.

"Captain!" a voice called from behind Gringar. Gringar stopped, and as he was about to look back to ask what was wrong, the blue moonlight glancing off the metal on the ground caught his eye. He pulled his horse up to the familiar armor strewn across the pathway and quickly dismounted his horse. His second in command, Grantham, dismounted his horse and knelt down beside the armor. He picked up a heavy breastplate, gold with a silver, curved sword moving diagonally across the surface of the armor.

"Do you recognize it?" Gringar asked Grantham.

"No," answered Grantham.

"Neither do I," said Gringar.

"Do you think one of our men was taken?" asked Grantham.

He took the breastplate and examined it. There was no sign of struggle. It would take a great fight to separate a Kiläl soldier from his armor. To do so would almost be like rendering the soldier naked. A Kiläl wore his armor to sleep even, being always and at all times prepared for battle. A Kiläl soldier was a soldier before he was anything else. To see a fellow soldier's armor on the ground was almost like seeing him dead. It unsettled all the Kiläl, as they pulled their horses up closer, looking at the strange scene. However, they all remained quiet, having been trained to keep their thoughts to themselves unless asked for them. But all of their minds turned back to the strange men that they had just met on the trail.

"I don't think so," answered Gringar. "I want the two men we just saw," he said as he took one of the smaller pieces of armor – a hand plate – off the ground and swiftly re-mounted his horse. He sized up the situation and decided to send Grantham ahead to the house with half of the men in case Mag was in need of help somewhere up ahead. All the possibilities of what could have happened ran through his mind as a new sense of urgency awoke within him. Mag was hurt or dead, the family they searched for was gone or at the house. He didn't know, but he sensed that something was amiss. With a certain swiftness, the two parties set out, each in their own direction— with their own purpose.

†††

As they rode through the depths of the forest as fast as they could go, Far noted that the night had become as dark as it could be. He could barely see the road as it came toward him. He trusted that Heiður's sight was clearer than his as he entrusted their journey to his stallion. He tried to understand what part of the path they were on. He sensed that the clearing that opened up to the bridge that crossed the Trinity River and led into Maisondepahn was up ahead, but it was only his senses that told him so. It was reason enough to move Heiður fast through the remaining part of the forest, if this was in fact the last of it.

"I think we might be coming to the plain of Tertunliguan," Far turned and yelled to Péttur through the wind that was pushing past them.

"Really?" Péttur asked. "How can you tell?"

"I don't know!" Far yelled, "I just feel it."

The moon had gone down below the horizon. He wished that it was still a bright light in the sky, as it had been not long before, Far thought to himself, but it is always darkest before the dawn, he was reminded. It was his first true spiritual father who had taught him that, he remembered. How true it had been throughout his life. Please let this be that time, he prayed. Please let Maisondepahn be that dawn.

Beyond his thoughts, he heard a voice... "Far, do you hear that?"

His heart sank. He had heard it. He hoped that it was just the sound of his heart beating fast or some animal in the forest, but no. He knew.

"Yes!" he yelled back to Péttur. "Hold on!" He clicked in Heiður's ear. The horse was hesitant to go faster in the darkness, but Far let him know that it was okay. The sound of Eiwengaard armor is easy to hear from distances far away— something that was meant to strike fear into the Kiläl's enemies, but certainly worked against them, at times, for other reasons.

"Can we out-run them?" Péttur asked.

"I don't know," answered Far truthfully.

"You can let me off," Péttur said. "Then you will be faster."

"Or you could let me off," Far answered.

"No." Péttur said. "They will be satisfied with me."

"We will stay together, Péttur!" Far answered finally, concentrating on the path. He thought that he could see a light up ahead. If they could just make it to the Beautiful Gate, they would be under the protection of the Royame. He concentrated his mind on the gate and suddenly, they were out of the forest and what starlight could illuminate the earth landed on the grass, seemingly illuminating the plain. It was lighter than the forest, anyway.

Far's eyes adjusted to the new scene. He could see the tall, white pillars that ascended at each side of the bridge opening. This was the only entry to Maisondepahn, as the city was built in the middle of a large piece of land that rested in the midst of a deep canyon. The city was surrounded as well by a great, white wall that was guarded by soldiers at all times. As soon as they saw him coming, he knew they would be safe.

He hit Heiður's sides lightly with a rope and clicked his tongue fast in his ear, leaning down into the wind. They were gliding fast through the plain when he felt another wind behind him. He looked back to see 6 Kiläl soldiers closing in fast. As they neared the bridge, Far looked for the Royameheir soldier that stood watch at the opening at all times. Not seeing one, he was a bit relieved. At least there would be no resistance there. But the guards at the top of the wall would surely see him. He removed his cloak so that they would recognize his sash and see that he was a saçèrdōté.

Heiður cut in and out of bushes, navigating his way deftly through the plain, sensing, Far thought, that he was almost home as well. It had only been days since they had been in Maisondepahn, but it seemed like years, Far thought. Surely Heiður was just as happy to be home as he was. In his heart, he was already there, surrendering his safety into the hands of his brothers who would certainly defend him against an entire Kiläl army, if need be.

As they neared the opening, the sun started to peak up on the edge of the horizon to their right. Always darkest before the dawn, Far smiled to himself. However, as they neared the opening of the bridge, something unusual presented itself to Far. It was a pile of metal that seemed to be lying next to the opening. As he neared the opening, he recognized the Eiwengaar armor and suddenly realized that there was a Kiläl soldier asleep inside it. His heart sank as he realized what this meant. Seeing the Beautiful Gate, he could not do anything but press forward toward it, though in his heart, he knew that there was no safety there. There simply was just no other place to go. He knew that the Beautiful Gate would not open for him, but there were other, secret gates in the wall that he hoped the Kiläl would not have found. There were tunnels, ancient as the Royame, that went below the river even and came out beyond the canyon, but they were impossible to open from the plain side, even for the Royame's most trusted sons.

The bridge was sturdy, made of concrete. It had been made of every expendable material, being burned or destroyed in other ways by the Royame during times of war, but eventually the counsel decided to make it of concrete and defend it in times of war so that it was safe for traveling across during times of peace, which was what it was mainly used for. Until the Kiläl soldiers had descended on the city four days ago, it had been fine. But it was a false security that allowed for the breach. The Kiläl, disguised as Royameheirs traveling from another country, came into the city during the Pax festival. How many there even were, no one knew. At an appointed time, they removed their swords and slaughtered the children. Because of the sorrow and the confusion and all of the people fleeing, most of the Kiläl were able to flee before anyone even realized what had happened.

"Had they returned to occupy the city?" Far wondered.

Péttur, being able to recognize Kiläl armor from miles away, says when he tells the story, that his mind went through every possible explanation for seeing that pile of metal there, except for the one that he knew in his heart was true, before he said, "Far," not being able to hide the disappointment of his heart.

Far nodded. "We're going over the bridge anyway," he yelled back to Péttur through the wind. Obviously, he thought to himself. Where else was there to go? "There are secret entrances in the wall!" he yelled back.

Some sliver of hope returned to Péttur's heart and he held onto it. They reached the entrance of the bridge. Far's heart regained momentum as he heard the familiar sound of Heiður's hooves beating against the concrete. He knew that Heiður felt it too. He picked up speed as he heard the clunking of Kiläl armor falling on itself as the soldier awakened. Gringar yelled at the soldier as he passed, pushing him to the ground in anger. The armor fell loudly to the ground, but got up as fast as it could to ring the warning bell.

Suddenly, the morning light glinted off of metal lining the wall just as Far and Péttur reached the edge of the bridge. It was as Far feared. The Kiläl had returned to occupy the mourning city. The soldiers were clearly confused by what they saw, but seemed to understand that one of their Kiläl was chasing the pair. Gringar shouted something up to the soldiers in their native tongue and bows were quickly drawn.

Far moved right and rode as fast as he could, staying as close to the wall as he could. He looked for the tree that signaled the place where the stone would become a door if the lever was pushed. Arrows rained down around them as the Kiläl horses closed in. He debated on whether to use the entrance in front of the Kiläl. They had already breached the city, he decided, and so thought that it would be okay, though it could weaken the city's defenses if there was a future attack. He would rather not, but he didn't see any other way. He used all of his focus to seek the lever, knowing that if he missed it there would only be a few more chances to enter the city.

He had not had time to think about what the consequences of his hiding inside the city walls would be, but, as he neared the gate, he understood that if the Kiläl were truly in control of the city, as it seemed, they would stop at nothing to find him and he could not think of a reason why his life was more important than the lives of the people in the city at this moment. If the Kiläl would slaughter all of the innocents of the city, then why would they hesitate to slaughter others to find him and Péttur. He knew their tactics well. He could envision, without hesitation, what would happen. He would give himself up anyway to save the lives of the people. Clearly, the Royameheir forces had somehow been subdued. His heart suddenly sank as he realized what he must do. Heiður, sensing his master's change of heart, began slowing down.

"What's happening?" Péttur asked.

"No one can take your life from you, Péttur," Far said. "Remember that, okay?"

"Okay," Péttur answered, hearing the understanding in his heart through his voice before his head had a chance to process it.

"Right now, offer your life, whatever happens, for the people of the city."

"The people I once persecuted myself," the breath of Péttur's voice spoke, seemingly without him. "Yes, Far, I offer my life for them," Péttur answered, wondering where the resolve in his heart and his voice was coming from. 'It must be the new heart in me,' Péttur thought.

"Good boy," Far said, slowly bringing Heiður to a full stop.

## Chapter 10

## Strong Wind

The man kept looking at me as the two parties, those who wished to keep us with them and offer us the protection of the tribe and those who wished for us to leave immediately, continued their debates.

Haddar rapped his fist against the table. He rapped it louder. Finally, he yelled, "Silence!"

The entire room fell silent at last. "The council has spoken. It is final," he said, but as he said it, his glance turned to Abu Atta, as though he wasn't sure about the words he was saying. Abu Atta met his gaze and looked down.

"Stephen, son of Chris," Haddar said, "I am sorry to tell you and your family that the protection of our tribe will not fall on you. According to our custom, you may eat a meal with us and then you must leave. "The sun is rising," continued Haddar, as he looked to a small place in the tent wall where the sun's light was breaking into the darkness of the council tent, "we will share first meal and then we will send you with full provision on your way."

I could tell that the tribesmen who wished for us to stay, including the man beside me, wished to say something, but they kept their thoughts to themselves and resignedly arose from the table, each now looking at us and offering my father a touch on the shoulder to let him know that they were with him, especially as fathers, which each of them were, who knew what it would be like to confront the desert, unprotected, with a baby.

One by one they arose from the table and filed out the tent door, letting a triangle of light enter into the room and illuminate us each time a body went through, blackening the triangle with its shadow. Soon, only Haddar was sitting with us at the table. He turned to my father.

"Stephen, if there was anything I could do..." he began, but my father stopped him.

"No, please let me continue," he said. "I will send two men to escort you through the desert. I cannot offer you the protection of the tribe, but I will see to it that you find your way to the Black City."

"I don't know where we are going," my father said, looking from me to my mother, "but I am glad for any help that you can offer." He managed a smile that was meant to comfort Haddar, who was clearly worried about what this would mean, not only for us, but for his tribe, if he was turning away someone who was meant to fall under their protection. He knew well the price that could be paid by the people if they did not do the will of their God.

"I will leave you alone to speak about the future," Haddar offered. "We will be preparing the first meal." "It will be special," he said, his voice cracking a little, "in honor of your family."

"Thank you," my father said, managing a small smile for Haddar's sake.

After Haddar left the tent, my father pulled us into his body, offering what comfort he could. "Well," he said, looking deeply into my mother's eyes, "the desert it is. The protection of the desert."

My mother looked trustingly into his eyes. "The protection of the desert," she repeated.

"You know that the desert has protected our people for millenia. So it will be for us. The design of the Royame is before us and we know that we are its children," he said to her. It seemed she already knew everything that he said, but the words needed to be said aloud.

"The Royame," my mother said gently, resting her head on his breast. We stayed like that for moments, gaining strength from each other's presence.

†††

The feast that the Atta Tribe prepared was truly magnificent. They had spared no expense in setting before us the best that they had to offer. Though the tribe was clearly in mourning for their loss – the women were all dressed in black and the sadness of their eyes was palpable – the combined sadnesses of the moment mingled with joy at a feast beautifully prepared and the hope that stirred in the hearts of the people as they sat at table with the Snake Destroyer. Haddar showed my mother and father to their places at the head of the table, seating them and me on their finest pillows. Gercek came to sit beside my father along with his wife and their children.

"I will travel with you to the Black City, friend," he said. "It is all in the hands of the Royame," he assured my father.

"Why the Black City?" my father asked.

"In the Black City you will go unnoticed. It is a large city. A family could stay there undetected for many years and it will have all that you need to make a living," Gercek said.

"I see," said my father, contemplating this new idea.

"You will like it," Gercek said, smiling. "You will see." He slapped my father on the back as men were wont to do to each other in this culture, I noticed.

"Why do they call it the Black City?" my mother asked.

"Oh yes," said Gercek. "It is not as foreboding as it sounds. There is black rock in abundance in the city. The whole town is built with it. There are great streams and rivers that flow beneath the city and come out of black fountains. I am sure you have heard of it," Gercek went on.

My father nodded that he had heard of it.

"And the buildings are the tallest you have ever seen. The black stone is very strong," he said proudly, as though it was his own.

"What are the people like?" my mother asked, pulling me close to her heart.

"They are people," said Gercek. "I need not tell you the nature of people, but there are some there who I know. They are good. I will show you who they are."

"King Maxamea's army?" asked my father.

"Of course, Stephen, but they are everywhere," answered Gercek.

"Everywhere but here," my father corrected.

"Yes, that is true," Gercek agreed, his disappointment showing itself in his face. My father put his hand on Gercek's shoulder to give him comfort. But there are your own people there, you know?" he said. "There are many of your own people there," he offered as a solace.

At this, my mother began to relax, I noticed, contemplating the presence of other Royameheirs.

"We will remain hidden, Gercek," my father said. "Even from our own people if possible." At this, Gercek's look changed to one of understanding.

"I see," he said. "Well, if it is hiding that you want, the Black City is your place."

Food was set before us, one plate after another, and people came to offer their well wishes. We accepted them graciously. Everyone touched my head or my hand and smiled their beautiful, white smiles at me, looked sweetly at me, but with a hint of curiosity mixed in, as though they were not sure what to think exactly, but they wished me well.

†††

The sun was beginning its ascent in the sky as I was handed up into my mother's hands. The tribesmen readied our horses and filled out bags with provisions enough to last us weeks, though the Black City was only a day's journey East. Gercek, along with two other tribesmen, mounted their camels. The entire tribe came to say goodbye to the Snake Destroyer and his family. Some wept. Some kissed my father's feet and mother's hands, some touched my face as though they would receive a blessing from it. They had taken palm leaves from the palm trees around us and fanned the heat away from our bodies.

  The crowd made way for a little man to pass through. Abu Atta approached my father. The crowd fell silent. The contents of this conversation were only known to my father at this time. Abu Atta did not want to incite unrest with the crowd. He asked my father to lean forward.

  "Stephen, son of Chris, you are the Snake Destroyer," he said, looking deep into his eyes. "And you are meant to be our savior and to bring about our destruction," he said. "But the council has spoken. I could have overturned their decision, but I did not. It is important to me that you know this so that you know what power I had and that I did not use it."

My father nodded, understanding how delicate it is to understand the will of God.

"But perhaps it is by leaving that you will fulfill your destiny. I must believe that and I welcome it. Whatever your destiny is, whatever it means for our people. I welcome it and I know that the will of our God cannot be undone, so if by sending you away, the people think they have protected our tribe from your destiny, I believe in fact that they send you away to fulfill it. My prayer goes with you wherever you are, Stephen son of Chris and your beautiful family," he said, touching his hand to my head to give his blessing.

When Abu Atta stepped away from my father, giving his blessing, the crowds moved back, as though they knew that no more could be added. The three camels started out into the desert and slowly the horses fell into step behind them. We did not fly in hopeful anticipation, as we had fled the edge of the forest, but we walked somberly into an unknown day to an unknown land.

As we crested the edge of the first dune that would take us out of sight of the tribe, we suddenly heard from a mile behind us the sounds of the tribe yelling. What they were yelling, we could not hear. We stopped and turned back toward the camp to see what they were yelling about. My mother thought that it was just part of their custom, but the questioning looks on the faces of our guides told us otherwise. They were pointing up into the sky.

We watched as Pålitlig came soaring toward us, having made his final swoop over the crowd behind us. As he approached, my eyes were on my father's face, which looked like it had seen a ghost. There was a writhing snake in Pålitlig's claws.

†††

"Far Larkin!" the people yelled, as they recognized Far's sash and followed Heiður, now tied to a Kiläl horse, to the jail where they meant to keep him. Gringar had covered Far's face, hoping that he would not be noticed, but the people noticed him anyway.

The officials of the city, who were neither Royameheir nor Kiläl, approached Gringar.

"What do you mean to do with the saçèrdōtés and this man?" asked the official, noticing Péttur, who was himself tied to a Kiläl horse.

"I am taking them for questioning," Gringar answered, knowing the government's love of questioning subjects, though the Kiläl never bothered with such things.

"What is their crime?" he asked.

They attacked one of our soldiers," Gringar answered.

The official looked at Far, who couldn't see him. "Is this true?" asked the official loudly.

"No," Far answered.

"You are not to cause these men any harm. They will be tried if they deny your charges," the official reminded Gringar.

"Your laws do not concern me," Gringar answered, as he pushed the official out of the way with his boot.

At this, the official's soldiers, who were apparently co-occupying the city, lifted their spears into the air and then brought them down hard on the ground in front of the Kiläl horses.

"Anyone who lives here is concerned with our laws," the official answered.

"They won't be harmed," Gringar huffed, and then added, "yet." as he yanked the horse's rein forward.

The crowd that tried to follow Far was kept back by the government officials and the Kiläl soldiers who came to lend their support to Gringar and the other Kiläl.

Péttur looked out on the crowd and noticed that the sympathy of the Royameheirs in the crowd fell on him, seeing that he was a penitent, one of their own. I wouldn't trade this moment to be in that armor on that horse for anything in the world, he thought to himself and renewed his promise to give his life to save these people if need be. It would not be for nothing, he reminded himself. It would be for them. I had a choice – to save myself or to save them and I chose them, he reminded himself. This is not for nothing. A whip came down hard on his head, its tip striking his cheak, bringing blood. "Hurry up!" the Kiläl soldier yelled. He forgave the soldier, as Far had taught him to do, and moved faster.

When they arrived at the jail, a Kiläl soldier told Far to get down off the horse.

"His legs are broken," Péttur said. Noticing that no one heard him, or Far, who was trying to explain, he yelled louder. "His legs are broken!" The sorrow in Péttur's heart re-kindled as he heard these words, remembering that it was his fault.

The whip struck Péttur again in the head.

"Shut up." the soldier said.

Péttur tried to tell the soldier who was hitting him. "His legs are broken."

The soldier laughed. "This should be good then."

"Off the horse, saçèrdōté!" Gringar yelled at Far.

"My legs are broken," Far explained again, but as the words were coming from his mouth, Gringar pushed Far off the horse with his boot.

Péttur's heart exploded as Far hit the ground. He moved toward him, falling over a soldier's foot and landing nearing his face. He looked at Far, who was trying not to cry out.

"I'm so sorry, Far," Péttur said.

Far smiled. "I'm not," he said as he opened his eyes and looked lovingly at Péttur. "Remember that," he said, "the next time you want to apologize."

At that, Péttur was lifted off the ground by a metal-covered arm. The soldier pushed him into a dark room where he could hear the soldiers telling Far to crawl if he couldn't walk.

Péttur wept with every call he heard the soldiers yell at Far.  He listened as the blows of their boots landed on Far's body. With each blow, a fresh wound was dealt Péttur, knowing that each blow was his own fault.  If he had not been so blind, if he had not faltered in the first place, if he had woken up when Far first reached out to him... with each blow, a fresh memory of his fallenness surfaced.  With each sorrow, he saw Far looking at him with those fatherly eyes, saying, "I'm not" and each time Far's mercy covered his own brokenness, his heart convulsed within his chest so that he thought that it would burst.

He welcomed the bars as they closed him into his own personal cell and he grasped the dirt floor, looking for something solid to hold onto.  His head was reeling from the pain he knew Far was experiencing.  He heard the soldiers spit on his body and yell obscenities at him.  He heard himself crying, "No.  No.  No." as the tears began to form a small pool of mud in front of him.

He waited and waited and waited to see Far's face come around the corner.  How long could they watch a lame man crawl?  How long would it take to drag his body to his cell?  Wouldn't they get tired eventually and just pick him up?  There was a bowl of water on the ground.  He decided to wash some of the mud from his face and body.  The water mixed with the tears on his face each time he heard the soldiers yell at Far. After he was done washing his face, there was nothing left to do but pray. He remembered that Far said the Lady would hear him if he spoke to her. He got on his knees. He stayed that way for what seemed like hours, pleading for Far's life.

Finally, a soldier walked into the room and opened the door of the cell next to Péttur. "Here comes the dog!" he yelled. "Make way for the poor dog. Look at the poor dog," he laughed, inciting a feeling in Péttur he had not felt since his heart was renewed — anger. He questioned the feeling and handed it over to his renewed heart. He found there pity where the anger tried to swell — pity for a man who was as blind as he once was. He saw himself in the man and love actually came to the surface. He locked eyes with him and the man, Péttur knew, saw the love, and he stopped calling out. He just held the door.

Péttur felt his body fly to the bars before his head knew what was happening. Far's weak body was making its way into the room. Péttur fell to his knees again in prayer since there was nothing else he could do. With each blow that the soldiers dealt him, Far drew in a breath and renewed, Péttur could see, his resolve to make it to the goal— his cell. Every time a blow came, he looked at Péttur and showed him a thing that only Péttur was able to see. Behind the pain, there was joy. The joy of suffering for the Royame— "a mystery," he had explained to Péttur, "to all who have not yet experienced it." Péttur tried to believe it. There was no way not to. It was there. The joy was in his eyes, as sure as the bloody marks that covered his back, tearing his beautiful saçerdōtan jacket to shreds.

    As it seemed Far was going to accomplish the task of arriving at the cell, the soldiers became further incensed and renewed their efforts, whipping him with the whip, kicking him with their boots. It seemed almost like they were possessed by a demon, the evil in them seemed so great. They didn't even seem human anymore. Four soldiers beat him ceaselessly all the way to his cell. Péttur's hands reached through the bars toward him as his body came almost within reach. It was all he could do for the man he loved, the man who saved his life, the man who gave him life again. There was not a hopelessness in his face. Far had given him the hope he needed.

    Once in awhile, Péttur saw a soldier look at him, the tears running freshly down his face. It seemed for a moment he could see the pain and the love in Péttur's eyes. Péttur could not find within himself the ability to judge any of the soldiers, seeing in himself the man who was holding the whip, the man whose boot was lodging itself in his ribs. The love that Far had for Péttur he felt coming through his own eyes and finding its mark in the soldiers' eyes.

The beating suddenly abated as Far lay in a pool of his own blood— his face covered, Péttur saw, in spit.

When the soldiers left, Péttur cried out to Far, "Come. Please come here. Please."

"No, Péttur," Far managed. "Just let me lay here."

Péttur couldn't stand it. "No, Far. Come here. Please. Please come here," he said.

For Péttur, Far found the strength to pull himself across the floor the three feet to the bars that separated his own cell from Péttur's.

As soon as Far was within reach, Péttur took the scarf from off of his neck and cleaned Far's face carefully with the cloth. He wet a clean part of the the scarf in the bowl of water and let Far drink from it, then took his hands in his own, and cleaned them to the best of his ability. He cleaned his face again with the water.

Far smiled. "Thank you, Péttur," he said. "Thank you, son," and lay his head heavily on the ground.

Péttur wept as he put his arms through the bars and pulled the jacket from the wounds of Far's back, removing the cloth from the inside of the red caverns the whips had cut into his body. As he dabbed the wounds with the cloth, freshly dipped in water, he wept. "I'm sorry," he said. "I'm so sorry." He just kept saying it over and over. He couldn't find anything else to say.

Far found the strength to pick his head up from the floor of the cell. The side of his face was covered in the soft dirt. As Péttur's hand wiped the dirt freshly from the wounds in his face, Far said, "Look at me, Péttur." Péttur could not look at him. Far found the strength to take Péttur's face in his hand and pull it toward him. He found his eyes. "I told you," he said. "I'm not." He smiled at Péttur with his eyes until the smile was returned and, as the last of his strength left him, his head hit the ground.

†††

As we travelled through the desert, safely under the protection of the three Amud Udi Aramad, and Pålitlig, a pain was thrust into my heart. I cried out. My mother, unaccustomed to my cries, looked at me. I saw the worry in her eyes. I wanted to stop that worry, but the pain in my heart was like a knife. I cried out for Far. I didn't know why, but I wanted him. I needed to see him. I needed to look at his eyes. The feeling was one that I will never forget. More than food when I was hungry, more than my parents, I needed to see him and I couldn't and there was no way to communicate to my mother what my need was. I know now that it was when Far fell from his horse that this feeling overtook me and would not leave. It was when he was being beaten by the soldiers. I would not be comforted. The rest of the trip to the Black City, for me, was one of pain. I remember the desert that we crossed to reach the Black City being one of hardship and pain, though nothing in our caravan had changed.

My mother stopped the caravan in the noon sun and unwrapped my body to find welps on it, as though something had struck me or stung me. She showed my body to my father, who was equally astonished. They looked at each other as they poured water over my body, not being able to think of anything else to do and then, finally, offered my body itself to the mysteries of the Royame. Gercek looked at my body and looked at my father. "Little Reina," he said. "Who she is we do not know," and then returned to his camel after pressing his forehead to mine. They went on, stopping to check my body periodically. For three hours, new welps formed on my skin. That was how long it took Far to reach the cell, I was later told – three hours in the hot sun of Maisondepahn, the same sun that hovered over our travelling bodies.

Suddenly, the pain stopped and I was exhausted. I fell asleep and my mother held me close to her, checking my body to see if the marks had disappeared with the crying. They had not. She took the softer veil from her head and wrapped my body in it. I remained like that for the rest of the journey to the desert's end. As the sun cooled, so did the wounds of my body become a dull ache, but nonetheless, I slept, waking only long enough to eat, feel the hot pains of my body in the hot sun, search the desert for my spiritual father, and then go back to sleep.

I awoke one such time, searched the desert, and found a sight that I had never seen before. The flaming sun suspended itself behind what looked like sand that had found its will to reach for the sun and blackened itself trying in a thousand different ways, in a thousand different shapes, to rise up from the earth. One form, like a tidal wave, rose from the center and eclipsed all the others, reminding me of a tall man with a pointed hat. A great shadow stretched toward us from the black forms that swept to the left and right as far as my eyes could see. I learned something of what it meant to be human in that moment, grappled with it, fought it momentarily because it so baffled my new eyes.

I didn't have the strength to try to understand what I was looking at, so I collapsed back into my mother's arms as the sun began to disappear below the Black City, calling forth, as I fell into unconsciousness, the cool wind, black in its nature too somehow, promising a safety as deceiving as it was sure.

Relieved worry was reflected in my mother's eyes as she looked down at me for the last time in the desert and then back to the Black City, finding the resolution within herself to walk forward into our new life in the world.

From the darkness of my mind, I heard the sounds of farewell – my parents saying goodbye to the Demudi Udi Aramad, except for Gercek, who would make introductions for us in our new home. I opened my eyes, wanting to see the strange shapes of the camels and the travellers again. I saw my mother instead. I had never seen that particular look of courageous resolution in her face. Her countenance struck me and I watched as she set her face like flint toward the Black City. I saw the very moment that she decided to walk forward, the sun's rays, parallel with the earth, creating fierce, blue diamonds in her eyes, and so she did. She walked forward.

It took, as all the previous moments had taken, a superhuman strength to do something so deceptively simple– the only thing that was left to do. She could have chosen death. It was really the only other choice, and as she would tell me later – the only choice less appealing than walking with her newborn babe into the enemy's seat, cloaked in a veil of mystery, drinking hope like a draught.

# Pronunciation Guide

Asa-ari    Assa-ah-ree
Asa-aul    Assa-ah-ool
Baekdu    Bayk-doo
Eiwengaard    Eye-ven-gahrd
Gercek    Gurr-sick
Haddar    Hay-dahr
Heiður    Hay-duhr
Kiläl    Kee-lahl
L'Agneau    Lag-nyoo
Letzē    Leht-zee
Maisondepahn    Maizohn-de-pan
Maxamea    Max-uh-may-yuh
Mezulari    Meh-zoo-lah-ree
Misr    Mee-zurh
Njardovik    Jar-doh-veek
Overlämnande    Over-lahm-nahnd
Pålitlig    Pah-leet-leeg
Péttur    Pay-turh
Riðiðafhinuilla    Ree-dee-dah-fihn-wee-lah
Roi    Ruh-wah
Royame    Roh-yum
Royameheirs    Roh-yum-errs
Saçèrdōté    Sass-hair-doh-tay
Tōb    toeb
Ukryty    You-kree-tee